THE
PEACEGIVER

THE
PEACEGIVER

*How Christ Offers to Heal
Our Hearts and Homes*

JAMES L. FERRELL

DESERET
BOOK

SALT LAKE CITY, UTAH

DESERET BOOK is a registered trademark of Deseret Book Company.

Visit us at deseretbook.com

Library of Congress Cataloging-in-Publication Data

ISBN 1-59038-223-4 (hardbound : alk. paper)

Printed in the United States of America   18961
R. R. Donnelley and Sons, Crawfordsville, IN

10   9   8   7   6

"I will take away the stony heart out of your flesh . . . "

—Ezekiel 36:26

CONTENTS

CONTENTS

PREFACE

We live in a world at war. I am referring not only to wars between countries but also between former friends, siblings, spouses, parents, and children. Conflicts between countries are perhaps more dramatic, but the hot and cold wars that fester in the hearts of family members, neighbors, and friends bring more pain and suffering to this earth in a single day than have all the world's weapons since the beginning of time. If there ever is to be peace on earth, we first must find the way to peace in our hearts and homes.

"I am the way,"[1] the Lord declared. "After your tribulation, I will feel after you," he promised. "And if you harden not your hearts, and stiffen not your necks against me, I will heal you."[2]

Nothing is more important than understanding not just *that* the Lord's atonement is the answer to our daily, painful predicaments, but *how* it is the answer. This book is an account of how the Lord "feels after us to heal us," and what we must do to receive the peace of his healing. It is the story of a husband and wife whose marriage is in trouble. It could just as well be the story of a father and child who aren't speaking, or of neighbors who bristle at each encroachment over a property line. The Lord's atonement reaches deep into the trouble of daily life to the very bottom of every dispute and hurt feeling. To the predicament of a hard heart, he offers the promise of a new one. To the pain of hurt feelings, he offers the balm of his love. To utter loneliness, he offers the companionship of the heavens.

His birth was heralded by the words "Peace, good will toward men"[3] because his atonement is what makes peace and good will possible. Whether in a home or a bunker, the way to true, deep, lasting peace is only in and through the Prince of Peace. "He *is* our peace," Paul declared, for through his atonement he has "broken down the middle wall of partition between us; having abolished in his flesh the enmity."[4]

There are far too many partitions in our hearts and homes and too much enmity between us. But the carpenter of Nazareth has constructed for us peace. My desire is to explore with you *how.*

PART I

THE GIFT
OF ABIGAIL

A STORM IN THE SOUL

The night was cold, in more ways than one. Outside, a heavy wind pounded thick raindrops against the windows. The eves above Rick Carson's bed creaked, as they always did in such windstorms, and he could hear the lawn furniture scraping slowly along the patio, as if each chair were reaching out in a futile attempt to grab a handful of concrete. At times it felt as though the house's wooden frame was bending, a movement Rick supposed he could have measured if he had either the inkling or the instruments to do so. He felt himself leaning heavier into his bed, perhaps in his own futile attempt to keep the house anchored to its moorings or in an equally futile attempt to moor *himself* to something solid.

Behind him lay his wife of twelve years. They were hugging their respective edges of the queen bed, she facing the window and Rick the wall, careful not to touch each other. It had been three days since they had spoken a word to one another except out of necessity—nearly as long as the rain had been pounding at their home. Rick lay awake, wondering what he had done to deserve this. *Our marriage is a sham,* he thought, despite what he considered to have been his best efforts. *There is no tenderness, no understanding.* He ached with despair.

Things had been so bad with Carol for so long that Rick could barely remember the good times. There had been some. In fact, during the early years of their marriage Rick had thought he was quite happy, and he had believed Carol to be as well. But the increasing unhappiness of the intervening years had called these early beliefs into question. Rick was no longer sure how happy he or Carol had *ever* been. His memories of the past and hopes for the future sagged under the weight of a depressing present.

Despite the cloud of unhappiness he felt enveloping his marriage, Rick had until then done his best to minimize and deny the problems. He survived by employing a kind of inner diversionary trick—by pushing from his mind thoughts of Carol, his marriage, and the injustices and pains that inhabited his inner chambers and by concentrating on other things. *Everything will be okay if I can only hang on,* he thought, as he did his best to put a happy face on their relationship. *Carol will come around.* But Carol hadn't "come around," and their relationship was only deteriorating the more.

As he lay there, Rick could sense something amiss in the patience he had been purporting to exercise. For the longer he exercised it the more bitter and impatient he had become. He felt not unlike the drug addicts and alcoholics who assuage themselves with the naive lie that "this hit or drink will be the last." His marriage was in trouble, and what frightened him most was that he wasn't sure he cared anymore.

Over the last five or so years he had shed many tears over the predicament he found himself in. One night, Carol had suggested that perhaps it would be better if he moved out for awhile. "The time apart might help us appreciate each other more," she had said. But her voice lacked conviction and rang hollow of hope. It was a voice Rick knew, for he heard it within himself as well.

Rick remembered that terrible night as he now lay listening to the storm. When Carol suggested he leave, it was like hell itself opened wide its jaws to give Rick an immediate and threatening view of what he had wanted to keep himself from seeing. He began to shake uncontrollably, and tears that felt like they originated in the marrow of his bones gushed from his eyes. The tears, shudders, and cries came in torrents. Just as one spasm of heartbreak would seem to pass and his body would start to settle, a new wave would burst from deep within him and his wailing would begin anew. He felt his hope for happiness, which he had clung to until that moment, slipping away with each teardrop. All the while, Rick recalled, Carol lay next to him, emotionless. She hadn't reached over to comfort him.

As he lay in memory, Rick could still feel the echo of those shudders within him. Things had calmed a bit between himself and Carol over the past eighteen months, but the bleak essentials of their relationship remained the same. He hadn't left as Carol had asked because, probably out of pity, she had withdrawn the suggestion. But her words still hung in the air between them—*"Perhaps we need to get away from each other . . . maybe that will help . . . "*

Rick knew better. With the indifference he was feeling within himself, he feared that he might *like* the time away— time away from demands, expectations, criticisms, and the weight of Carol's unhappiness that pressed upon and accused him whenever they were together. Even worse, Rick was afraid Carol might like the time away as well—a risk with implications he couldn't bear to think about.

The streetlight in front of their house cast enough glow through the storm and against the wall Rick was facing to illuminate the painting of the two of them that hung there. The artist had captured Carol perfectly, he thought, from the straight line in which she set her mouth, to the determination in her jaw and the icy glare of her eye. *Even the painter couldn't deny it,* he thought to himself, feeling all the more discouraged. *Why didn't I see it before we married?*

2

MEMORIES

R ick and Carol were both members of The Church of Jesus Christ of Latter-day Saints—the "Mormon Church," as it was nicknamed by early antagonists. They had been married in one of the Church's holy temples, this one in Los Angeles. Temples differ from ordinary church buildings in that they are set apart solely for the delivery of sacred ordinances pertaining to "eternal families"—the idea being that families can be sealed together as family units into the eternities, each family joined to the generations that preceded it, until all of the worthy members of the human race are sealed up as the family of God.

Rick and Carol had been taught from their earliest days that marriage in the temple by one with the priesthood authority to seal couples beyond death and into the eternities was the crowning ordinance of their faith and the single most important decision of their life. So they did not take marriage lightly. When they entered the temple that late spring day, they believed they were starting something that would last forever.

Like many young men of his faith, Rick had served a mission for the Church for two years—two years away from school, work, and dating, during which time he did nothing but teach people about his beliefs. He had been home from his mission for less than a year, and was dealing with being dumped by his "dream girl," when he saw Carol for the first time.

It was the first day of the new semester at UCLA. Rick was sitting against the far wall of the Institute classroom—a religious studies course for members of the Mormon faith (and for young Mormons, a great place to meet potential dating partners)—when she walked in, looked around uncertainly, and took her seat on the other side of the room. She was tall, with dark brown, slightly wavy hair about shoulder length. Trim, athletic, and very pretty, physically she reminded Rick of Glenda, his ex-dream, and he looked at her almost in mourning. But as he stole glances in the new girl's direction, he saw something different in her. She seemed less assured of herself than Glenda had been. He could tell by the way her eyes darted to others in the room, as if wondering what they were thinking of her. Glenda would never have done that, he thought to himself. Believing that everyone was looking at her, she would have sat regally still, trophy-like, showing them what they had no hope of ever winning.

Rick's eyes had lingered on the new girl as he thought of this, and she busted him—meeting his gaze with her own. He looked quickly away, forcing himself to focus on the instructor, whose words had been nothing but muffled background noise to that point. Still, he could see the girl out of the corner of his eye and finally succumbed to the urge to again look in her direction. He resolved to find a way to meet her.

She left too quickly for him to catch her that night, but Rick sat next to the door two nights later, right behind where she had sat on Tuesday. Sure enough, she walked in again, alone, right before the class started, and sat in front of him.

He didn't hear much of that lesson either.

He introduced himself after class. Her name was Carol Holly Adamson. She had grown up in Bakersfield, the fourth of an enormous brood of thirteen children. She had returned that semester after two years off to work and save money for her school expenses. She was a twenty-two-year-old sophomore.

Her shyness, Rick discovered later, was due in part to the poverty in which she had been raised. She had also lost considerable weight in the previous year and looked better than she was accustomed to looking. She was now a first-rate beauty without the attitude Rick had come to expect from many who looked as she did. He fell for her immediately.

Their courtship had been lightning quick by L.A. standards— six months to engagement, another three to marriage. Eleven months later, their first child, Alan, was born. Another child,

Eric, came three years later, followed a few years after that by two girls born just fifteen months apart—Anika, now five, and Lauren, who was three. The children had added some of the pounds back to Carol that she had lost before Rick had met her, and although at times he longed for the athletically trim girl from the Institute class, he still found her attractive, even with all the trouble they had been having. If there was a problem in the physical attraction department, it was that Carol found his thinning hair and increasing waistline unattractive. The sparks were long gone, and he resented her for it.

The children were Rick's pride and joy. They were wonderful kids, if a little too prone to teasing, which Rick easily dismissed in light of his own childhood memories. "They're just kids," he had protested to Carol on a number of occasions, when it seemed to Rick she was taking too hard of a line. "Ease up a little." But in Rick's view of things, she never eased up enough. She harped on the children the way she harped on him, especially the boys. "Clean this." "Empty that." "You didn't do enough of this." "Why don't you care about that?" "When will you start thinking of others?" and so on. No positive reinforcement, no grateful recognition, no thanks—just buckets of worries, insecurities, and complaints.

Rick tried to spend frequent and quality time with the kids, partly to compensate for what he thought was Carol's lack of positive attention and partly to bury himself in relationships of unquestioning love. "Every child deserves a dog," a friend had once told him, "because puppies love their child masters no matter what has happened at school." To Rick, his children were his puppies. They ran to him when he arrived home, begged him to play, and enjoyed resting in his arms. Their warm and buoyant affection kept him afloat. It also, however, ripped him apart. *If they knew their parents' feelings,* he thought, *they wouldn't survive it; they'd be devastated and scarred for life.* His heart ached for them.

If not for the children, and for the social ramifications of divorce—both familial and in the Church—Rick was no longer confident he would still be married. He was teetering at the edge of an unthinkable abyss, an abyss with eternal implications and complications, and not just for him.

The thoughts were too painful, so he did what he always did—he tried to think of other things, the way one of his friends foolishly tried to think of other things when he began to feel the Spirit, in order not to cry. Rick closed his eyes and tried to force his way to sleep—an hour-long process or so, interrupted by frequent glances at the alarm clock to see how much time had passed.

Finally, he gave up, rolled to his back, and began to think of one of his heroes—his Grandpa Carson.

Grandpa Carson had been dead for ten years, and his death had been very difficult for Rick. They had grown close through Rick's childhood and teenage years, as he often spent extended periods during the summer months with Grandpa and Grandma on the farm. Sometimes Rick's younger sister and brother would join them, but very often it was just Rick and his grandparents for days and sometimes weeks at a time. During those periods, Grandpa taught him how to fish, how to golf, how to care for horses, and, perhaps more than anything, how to care for a wife. For Grandma Carson was notorious in the family for being an impossibly difficult woman. She was the best grandmother anyone could ever hope for—doting over her grandkids and complimenting them from sunup to sundown. But she was a very different person toward Grandpa. It seemed he couldn't do anything right. It was always "Dale this" and "Dale that." She put him down mercilessly, from his poor driving (even though *she* was the one who had backed over gas pumps on more than one occasion), to his few strands of hair that he combed proudly over his otherwise bald pate, to the way he had lied to a couple of robbers about money he said he wasn't carrying (a falsehood she quickly made the robbers aware of). She delivered most of her jabs with a smile, almost as if she were joking. But the sheer volume of her comments must have taken a terrible toll. Rick and the other grandchildren always marveled at the magnanimous way Grandpa reacted. He would wink to the nearest grandchild, and his eyes would twinkle as he drawled "Oh, Grandma" in apparent mock protest. He didn't seem to take her seriously when she talked that way, playing her comments as if she were merely having fun and giving the grandchildren the cue to read them the same way. After years together it was almost like the two of them had perfected a stand-up comic routine, Grandpa playing Laurel to Grandma's Hardy.

But Rick knew it wasn't quite that way, for he was seated between his grandparents during a ride back to the farm one warm summer evening when Grandpa lost his twinkle and forgot his wink. Rick was about nine years old at the time. Grandma had been badgering Grandpa about something and Grandpa suddenly lost his temper. "Oh, go to hell!" he blurted in disgust.

Rick sat stunned as they continued home in silence, for he had been raised to believe that swearing was taboo. He felt like the proverbial elephant in the middle of the room that no one dared acknowledge. When they arrived at the farm, Rick went straight to his room. From his bed he listened to them argue about how Grandma treated Grandpa around the grandkids.

The anger and argument didn't diminish his grandfather in Rick's eyes but rather enlarged him, for he knew that Grandpa was hurt by Grandma's negative comments but seemed to be able to love her all the same. And for the rest of his days, he never again lost his twinkle or forgot his wink. At least, not in front of Rick.

Over the past few years, Rick had thought often of his grandfather. More and more he found himself feeling that he had married a younger version of his grandmother. He thought of Grandpa and his example of perseverance as a way to survive. At times he had the feeling that his grandfather was watching him from wherever he was. This thought had often acted as a brake on Rick's worst impulses and helped him make the best of his unhappy situation.

Somewhere in the middle of these thoughts, Rick drifted into the sleep he had been searching for. As he settled into slumber, his memories constructed themselves around him, and he found himself in his grandfather's farmhouse.

3

MARCHING TO CARMEL

Dinner was cooking, and the aroma of homemade chicken noodle soup, his grandmother's specialty, wafted through the air. Rick looked for his grandmother but she was not around. He looked out the bay window and across the fishing pond to the pasture beyond. His grandfather Carson was standing in the middle of the pasture, a good four hundred yards away, looking toward the house. Rick knew instinctively that he was waiting for Rick to join him. He eagerly sprang from the house and started down the dirt path to the fields below.

The sights around Rick flooded him with memories—the pond just below the house where he had caught his first fish, the stream that drained from the pond and had been the site of many "twig races" between his cousins and him, the rolling mounds of the pasture that had created challenges when he was moving sprinkler pipe but had enabled so much snow-mobiling fun during the white of winter. This was Rick's favorite of all places—the open space and wonder of his childhood.

"How's my golf partner?" his grandfather asked with familiar jocularity when Rick reached him. He was wearing his trade-mark golf shirt, khaki pants, and tennis shoes—his "work clothes." These clothes were part of the family lore, both because he never seemed to change them (or else had multiple pairs of the same outfit) and because, for a rancher, he was remarkably ill-suited for hard labor. Much to Grandma Carson's chagrin, he invested heavily in hired hands and was usually the first to suggest an alternative to chores when his grandchildren were visiting. He retained his love for youthful adventures almost to his dying day. He looked as Rick remembered him, although without his usual glasses. "I'm fine, Grandpa," Rick lied.

"How's Carol?"

"Oh, she's fine too," he lied again, feeling a bit uneasy.

Grandpa Carson looked deeply at Rick. "And the kids?"

"Oh, they're great, you'd be real proud of them," Rick responded enthusiastically, grateful for a question he could answer honestly and with little effort. "Alan has a lot of *you* in him, Grandpa. Right down to his distaste for hard labor," he added, jokingly.

Grandpa Carson smiled pleasantly, but did not burst into

the ear-to-ear grin Rick remembered so fondly and had hoped to elicit.

Grandpa Carson rested his eyes on Rick without saying a word, and Rick's discomfort grew. He felt compelled either to turn away or to speak over the unease he was feeling.

"He and Eric are good young men," he blurted, choosing to do the latter. "Fun loving, but serious about serious things—well, for preteens anyway." Grandpa Carson again nodded pleasantly, still saying nothing.

"And the girls!" Rick exclaimed, over-talking the way one does when wishing to avoid other topics. "Anika and Lauren are little angels. They just make me smile."

"Yes, Ricky," his grandfather interjected. "They make me smile too."

"But you—"

"Never knew them?" Grandpa Carson responded.

Rick nodded sheepishly.

Grandpa turned his head and gazed off into the distance. He squinted ever so slightly, which creased his skin from the corners of his eyes to beyond his temples. To someone who didn't know him, this mild squint would seem merely an attempt to focus on a distant object. But Rick knew better. This, like the beaming smile Rick had hoped to see, was a look he recognized. His grandfather was focusing his thoughts more than his vision. Something was on his mind, and Rick was afraid he knew what it was.

"Do you remember the time we mowed the weeds on that little peninsula on the lower pond and made it into an island green?" Grandpa Carson asked, nodding toward the lake in the southeast corner of the pasture.

"Yeah, I remember," Rick chuckled, relieved by the question. It had taken them nearly all day to cut down the grass to the nubs and rig up a flagstick—a project they had embarked on instead of moving sprinkler pipe. Grandma wasn't very happy about it.

"Do you remember your hole-in-one that day?"

Did he ever! Rick had told the story so many times before, with such pride, that over the years he had forgotten to feel bad about the three-foot diameter hole they counted as the cup. "I'll never forget it, Grandpa."

"Do you remember how happy you were?"

"Oh yes, absolutely. I think I smiled for a solid week."

"Me too, Ricky," his grandfather agreed. "That was a great time."

He paused for a moment remembering the day. Then he turned back to Rick.

"Are you that happy now, Ricky?"

Despite his foreboding worries that the conversation might turn this direction, the question caught Rick short. He wanted so badly to say "Yes," but the best he was able to do was an unconvincing, "Yeah, I think so."

He dropped his eyes toward the ground, betraying all that his words had tried to keep hidden.

"I've been watching you, Ricky. I ask for reports as often as possible, and occasionally I am even allowed to check in on you. You make me so proud, Son." (He often called Rick "Son," and Rick loved it when he did.) "You're a hard worker, and a great father. But I know something of the struggles you are going through as well—both because I see them and because I've been through some of them myself. You've been in my prayers for years, and never more so than now. There are many who are praying for you, my boy."

Rick stood in silence, halfway between embarrassment and gratitude. *So Grandpa knows*, he thought to himself, resignedly, *he knows.*

Rick cut the charade. "I don't know what to do," he lamented. "Things are pretty rough right now, to tell you the truth. I've done everything I can think of, but nothing helps."

"I know, Ricky. I know. But there are a few things you haven't thought of. And the most important of those will not be something you do, but will rather be something you allow to be done *to* you."

"What do you mean?"

His grandfather smiled. "Come, I want to show you something."

Suddenly, Rick found himself on the top of the range of hills that ran along the eastern border of the ranch. He and his grandfather were standing next to the enormous boulder that towered like a sentinel on the "bald spot" of the mountain—the very highest point on the range and the destination of many horseback rides during his youth. From that vantage point, looking westward, he could see the whole of the ranch, with its pastures, lakes, and forests. The farmhouse was a tiny dot, but he could see it, along with the pond in front. From this height, the roof of the barn was visible from behind the huge cottonwoods that normally shielded it from view. Far below, at the base of the hill, flowed the Squalim River, where Rick and his family had played so often—fishing, camping, and floating on inner tubes through the gentle rapids.

"Come, Ricky," his grandfather said, putting his arm around Rick's shoulder and turning him from the view of the ranch. "I want you to see something." He walked Rick to the top of the bald spot to look out toward the east. To Rick's surprise, they looked down upon a vast desert wilderness. "I never saw this view before," he said. "Has it always looked this way?" But his grandfather didn't answer. *Did I ever look to the east of the range?* Rick asked himself. He couldn't remember.

Immediately below them spread a desert plain. From his vantage point high on the mountain, Rick could see far in every direction. To the north, the plain rose gradually on the backs of rounded hills. Southward, however, the sands continued as far as the eye could see, with rugged peaks thrusting heavenward here and there in the far distance. Twenty or so miles to the east, the plain fingered its way into a bleak and foreboding region of medium-height mountains. The fissures and cracks in the barren hills made the whole area look like it had been baked in a kiln. Through a few of those cracks, Rick could see beyond the hills into a deep, lake-filled valley that shimmered in the distance.

"Grandpa, has the land always looked like this?" Rick tried once again.

"Yes and no, Ricky," he answered. "The land has looked like this for millennia, but no, you have never seen it from here before."

"I don't understand."

Grandpa nodded but said nothing. He seemed to be waiting for something.

"Look," he said finally. "David and his men approach."

Rick squinted in the direction his grandfather was pointing, toward the northeast. Far below on the desert plain Rick could make out what appeared to be an area of scrub brush. But as he looked closer he saw the brush was moving. "David?" he puzzled aloud, unsure who his grandfather was talking about.

"Yes, look."

Rick suddenly found himself in the desert valley among a group of men, about six hundred in number. Dust clung to their clothes, which for most of them consisted of a roughly hewn outer garment that reminded Rick of what he had seen offered by street vendors on trips to Tijuana. The robes were fastened around their waists with thick leather belts. Smaller, lighter, pieces of cloth were draped over their heads and bound by a cord; these were close in color and weight to the undergarment that showed through rips and holes in their robes. Their beards were full and wild, their leathery faces and hands chaffed and dry. Rick couldn't help thinking that their skin resembled the baked terrain he had witnessed moments before from the ridge. They looked like vagabonds from Old Testament days who had been living in the wilderness for years without the tempering influence either of civilization or of gentle women.

Rick soon discovered this was precisely who they were.

A party of ten or so men approached the multitude, and the crowd parted, allowing them to move into the center of the throng. There Rick saw a most magnificent looking, strapping man. There was a dignity about him that set him apart both from the other men and from the terrain about him. It was obvious from his skin, clothing, and beard that he had been living this way at least as long as the others, but something was different about him, almost like his soul remained moist where others' had long been parched. Rick then noticed that the man's clothing, while every bit as dusty and worn as that of the others, seemed to be made of finer material. Rich colors peeked through the dust. *He belongs in other places,* Rick thought to himself, *loftier places. This is not his home.*

The approaching party stopped before the man. "David,

son of Jesse, we have been to the house of Nabal," spoke the man in front.

David, son of Jesse! thought Rick. He looked inquiringly at his grandfather. "Yes, Ricky," he said, as though reading his mind, "this is David, son of Jesse, future king of Israel."

"It is as you thought, my lord," said the spokesman, whose voice pulled Rick's attention back to the scene. "Nabal's shearers have gathered their plenty back to Carmel and they are making merry and feasting." The crowd of men, who were now gathering around the party of ten, nodded their heads happily and smiled their baked lips in approval.

"But he denies that he knows you, my lord. He refused to recognize our service to his men and his property. He mocked us and rejected our request for provisions. We have returned with nothing."

At this, the crowd erupted in anger. "This is an outrage," shouted a man to Rick's right. "He should pay for this, rejecting the son of Jesse," shouted another, shaking his fist angrily. The crowd howled their approval, and others began to shout further incendiaries. They began to stir each other into a rage.

"What is going on here, Grandpa?" asked Rick.

"The twenty-fifth chapter of First Samuel," he said. "Perhaps you have been golfing a little too much," he added, his eyes dancing playfully.

"David and this group of outcasts have been forced into the wilderness for survival," his grandfather continued. "After David

THE GIFT OF ABIGAIL

slew Goliath, his fame steadily climbed throughout the land. King Saul became insanely jealous of him and for years has been trying to kill him. David has lived the life of a vagabond, and these men, mostly fugitives from the law and outcasts from society, have gathered to him in the wilderness. We are now in the deserts south of Judea, in an area known as the wilderness of Paran. The body of water you noticed in the distance a moment ago was the Dead Sea.

"While here, David and his men have been protecting the shepherds and flocks of a rich man named Nabal. Bedouin tribesmen frequent these parts, and without protection many of Nabal's sheep would have been lost. David and his men could have fallen upon Nabal's flocks for their own sustenance, but they didn't. Neither did they take for themselves what the flocks and their handlers needed. Nabal's shearers have now gathered back to the Judean town of Carmel, to Nabal's estate, to shear and celebrate their plenty, and as you can see, David and his men remain here in need. Their provisions are running short."

"Despite this—despite all their help in enabling Nabal's plenty—he is refusing to help them?" Rick asked indignantly.

"Yes."

"No wonder they're outraged," Rick muttered.

Rick turned back to the men, who were yelping and waving their fists in the air around David. Since the word from his men, David had stood still, his countenance fallen to the earth.

Rick looked at him through the crowd. He had been stung by the report of Nabal's rebuff, to be sure, but appeared now to be regaining his composure. Rick could see the tension rising in his face as his men shouted around him. David's eyes narrowed and all at once seemed to fill with resolve. He flung his arm overhead, holding erect a long steel blade that glistened in the sunlight. "Gird ye on every man his sword,"[5] he shouted above the clamor. "We are going to Carmel to pay our respects to a fool named Nabal."

The men went wild. And among those men Rick suddenly noticed a man who could have been his twin. He, with the rest, was cheering wildly, his sword in hand.

Startled, Rick watched as David commanded a third of the men to stay with the meager provisions and then organized the remaining four hundred or so, Rick's twin included, for a march to Carmel. As he watched, Rick suddenly understood that the man was not his twin but himself. *He* was marching to Carmel with David. *But why?* He wondered. *What am I doing in this dream?*

The procession headed north toward the hills, kicking up the dust of the desert floor. When the trail of dust finally disappeared around the rise of a hill, Rick turned to his grandfather.

"Why have you shown me this, Grandpa?" he asked. "Why are we here? And why did I see myself among David's men?"

4

SOULS AT WAR

Y ou saw *yourself?*"

"Yes."

"Interesting," his grandfather said, glancing back in the direction the army had gone, as if pondering the revelation. "And perhaps fitting as well."

"Fitting? Why?"

"Because I'm afraid you are marching to Carmel, my boy."

"Well, yes, I am. I just saw me go."

"No, I don't mean merely here, Ricky. I mean at home as well."

"Huh?"

There was a long pause before Grandpa Carson responded.

"Ricky, I'd like to share with you something you may not know, at least not fully."

"Okay," he responded cautiously.

"Do you remember my brother, Uncle Joe?"

"Yeah, sure. He died in the rollover accident a few years before—"

Rick caught himself, because he was about to say "before you died," which seemed both impolite and oddly incorrect given the circumstances. "That is, he died about fifteen years ago, as I remember. The three of us played golf together a couple of times. You were really close to him; I remember that—fishing buddies and the like."

"Yes, but it wasn't always so, and that's what I'd like to talk to you about. My parents died some twenty years before you were born, leaving Joe and me alone. Of course, we were each parents ourselves by that time, and although it was a terribly sad period, we were able to move on fairly well. Until, that is, we came to the will and the dividing up of the estate.

"Joe was the oldest and expected the ranch to be his, as did I. Or if not, we thought it might be divided between us in some way. But Mom and Dad left it to me—*all* of it. Joe received other things, some of them quite valuable, but the loss of the ranch was a terrible blow to him.

"At the time, I wasn't sensitive enough to the situation. I didn't think about what it must have been like for him, the oldest boy, to lose his 'birthright,' as it were, to question in retrospect his love and relationship with his mother and father. Silently, I cheered my good fortune. I loved that grand place.

THE GIFT OF ABIGAIL

And secretly, I began to feel that I deserved it anyway. I, after all, was the one who moved back to help my father on the farm when he hurt his back, and so on and so on. Your grandmother and I moved our family onto the ranch within three months.

"As the months went by, Joe and I had a couple of blow-outs over the estate. He took some of the horses he had been given off of the ranch and started boarding them elsewhere. We started fighting over trinkets that we each thought had been promised to us. He stopped paying into our family trust fund that was to help fund missions and colleges for our children and grandchildren, and he began to speak badly about me to many of our mutual friends and acquaintances."

"Well, it doesn't sound like you did anything wrong, Grandpa."

"That's what I kept telling myself too, Ricky. But if that's true, if I did nothing wrong, then why didn't Joe and I speak for fourteen years?"

"You didn't speak for fourteen years?" This *was* something Rick hadn't heard.

"No. And neither did the families. Your father, he didn't see his cousins for probably two decades. Joe didn't even come to his wedding."

"But that wasn't your fault, Grandpa. You just followed your parents' wishes. It sounds to me like it was Uncle Joe's fault."

"*Did* I follow my parents' wishes, do you think, Ricky? Do

you think they wished for nearly two decades of estrangement between their boys?"

"But the *land,* Grandpa. You didn't do anything wrong."

"Ah, again, just what I had been telling *myself.* But over time I came to realize that I needed to look more deeply. There are ways to be right on the surface and entirely mistaken beneath. That was what the Savior announced to the world. 'The law, alone, cannot save you,' he said. 'I require the heart.'[6] He reserved his most blistering criticism for the most outwardly correct people of the day, the Pharisees, whom he accused of being 'whited sepulchres'—beautiful, law-abiding, 'in the right' on the outside, yet entirely corrupt within.[7]

"I am ashamed by the years I spent away from my brother—and for my feelings toward him during that period. Even if I was right on the land issue, and I'm not sure I was right even there, my heart warred toward Joe for years. And that, Ricky, can never be right. My parents did not bequeath me a warring heart. I took that upon myself."

He paused for a moment and shifted his weight. "There's something else I've been ashamed of, Ricky."

Rick waited.

"Many years ago, when you were quite young, I said something I shouldn't have in front of you. I blew up at your grandmother. I've regretted it ever since. I've hoped that the memory would fade from your mind, but have worried it's the kind of memory that never will."

Rick wanted to deny the memory, but he couldn't in the face of his grandfather's sincerity. "Yeah, I remember, Grandpa," he said sheepishly, not volunteering that he listened to the ensuing argument as well. "But it wasn't your fault," he added, trying to help. "I knew that then and *still* know it. To tell you the truth, I'm amazed that I only heard it from you once."

"Then my worst fears have been realized, my boy. It would have been better if you had blamed me all these years."

"*What?*"

"Look, you've been blaming Grandma, haven't you?"

"Well, no, not really," Rick offered flatly.

"No? But you thought my anger was warranted. You just said so yourself."

"Well, yes, I guess that's right. I saw the verbal beating you took every day. You were always so patient—had the patience of Job, in fact. So who could blame you if you blew up once. Who wouldn't?"

Grandpa sighed heavily, and to Rick he appeared to wither a bit, as if the desert heat was finally too much. But that wasn't it.

"I've done you a terrible disservice, my boy. When you think of me and your grandmother now you think of patience," he said, shaking his head and kicking at a rock. "Don't you know how much I loved her?"

"Well, sure, you *must* have to have put up so well with some of the things she did."

"Oh, dear boy, I have hurt you. I pray you will forgive me."

"Forgive you, Grandpa? For what?"

"For playing the part of a martyr so well that I undercut your love for your grandmother. For teaching you that 'patience' is possible in the face of difficulty but that love is not. For misleading you about love and its source."

"You didn't do any of those things."

"I'm afraid I did, and the reason why is clear to me now, as is the reason why I was chosen for this assignment."

"What assignment? What are you talking about?" But his grandfather ignored the question.

"So you saw yourself among David's men, Ricky?"

Rick nodded.

"If I had paid more attention," his grandfather continued, "perhaps I would have noticed a young Grandpa Carson as well. You see, when I suggest that you may be marching with David and his men not just here but also at home, I say it only because I too have marched to Carmel in my life, my heart gird for battle, my soul filled with war. And marching on that road as long as I did—both toward my brother and I'm afraid toward your grandmother as well, with devastating effect as I now see—I know where it leads. Believe me, Ricky, it is not a place you want to go."

He paused for a moment. "You see Carol as you think I saw Grandma, don't you?"

Rick hesitated. He didn't quite know how to answer.

"What I mean is that you saw Grandma do things to me that you didn't like. You saw her treat me poorly. And my explosion that night in the car rewrote in your mind my love for her into something it probably too often was: martyr-like patience. You thought I viewed Grandma as someone to be endured, someone toward whom deep love was not possible and outward civility was the most that could be hoped for or expected. Am I right?"

Rick didn't say anything, but he was starting to simmer inside.

"Is that who your Carol has become to you?"

The litany of Carol's faults and unkindnesses flooded through Rick's mind. "I guess I don't know what it was like to live with Grandma," he said, "but I'm having a real tough time with Carol. Yeah, you're right. She isn't who I thought she would be. She makes everything difficult. All things considered, I think I would be happy with patience—well, not happy, actually, but satisfied that I've done as well as I could. But I'm not even sure I can do that anymore. I'm afraid I'm nowhere near the man you were, Grandpa."

"And I'm afraid you are almost exactly the man I was.

"Ricky, listen," his grandfather continued. "I know Carol has mistreated you. That's what we do to each other—all of us—we mistreat each other, and especially those we live with, for we have more opportunities to mistreat them than anyone else. With respect to Grandma, by the way, you give me way too much credit and her far too little. Perhaps your young eyes weren't tuned to the more subtle forms of mistreatment I specialized in. Golfing instead of working takes its own toll, you know." He paused to let that settle.

"Ricky, I'm going to suggest something to you that you probably have never thought of and will want to resist, but I'm going to say it anyway because it's the truth. Here it is: Being mistreated is the most important condition of mortality, for eternity itself depends on how we view those who mistreat us."

Grandpa Carson paused at that, perhaps to emphasize the point.

"And that, Ricky, is why we are here in the wilderness of Paran. David and his men have been mistreated, as you have seen. They are marching off to war, their swords as well as their anger girded about them. You are with them, for you too are warring against mistreatment. But they, and you, are going to encounter someone on the march to Carmel—someone on the Lord's errand who changes mistreatment forever.

"Look!"

5

A PEACE OFFERING

The scene shifted again and Rick found himself on an out-cropping of rock, his grandfather by his side. A well-traveled path, fifteen feet or so in width, climbed up the side of a long hill to their left. The path passed before them no more than twenty yards away. It continued down to their right for some three hundred yards before it began to climb again and finally curved out of sight behind the hillside they were standing on. The slopes around them were covered with sagebrush and sprinkled here and there with wildflowers. An occasional scraggly tree forced its way toward the sky.

The warm air was still, and the afternoon sun was casting their shadows over the ledge on which they stood. There was nothing to see but the gentle road before them. Rick threw a questioning look toward his grandfather, who just nodded and smiled. Within a minute or so, Rick heard a *clop clop clop* coming from the top of the hill to their left, and he saw first one donkey, and then another, and another, until fourteen donkeys were descending the path, each laden with goods and being led by menservants. A little way behind them came another donkey, this one carrying a rider. As the procession approached, Rick could see that the rider was a woman dressed in beautiful robes, a veil covering the lower half of her face. She looked to be someone of importance.

"Who is this, Grandpa?" Rick asked.

"A most extraordinary woman," was his reply. "Her name is Abigail. She is Nabal's wife. One of the servants who overheard Nabal's harsh treatment of David's men reported to her what Nabal had done. She quickly set out to gather everything that David's men had asked for and more—foodstuffs and essentials that she could take to David before he acted against Nabal and his house, as Abigail worried he might. Among other things, she gathered bread, wine, dressed sheep, corn, raisins, and hundreds of fig cakes, packed them on donkeys, and set out upon this road to intercept David."[8]

Rick looked back at the woman. *How mistreated you must be too,* he thought to himself, imagining her life of trial with Nabal. With his own difficult marriage souring his soul, he felt an immediate kinship with her.

Just as she was passing before him, the procession stopped. The servants stared down the path to Rick's right, reporting their observations back to Abigail. Craning for a better look, Rick could make out an army approaching around the bend. It was David and his men.

Abigail dismounted and strode quickly past the donkeys and to the front of her servants, where she bowed herself to the ground facing the approaching army.[9]

David in his dusty splendor continued his approach, his men marching behind him. Their swords flashed in the sunlight as a cloud of dust trailed off behind them. Rick strained for a sight of himself in the crowd but couldn't find him. The army climbed the road until they were no more than fifteen yards from the bowing woman. David raised his right arm and halted his troops. He then strode forward and stopped before her.

Without looking up she crawled to David's feet.

"Upon me, my lord, upon me let this iniquity be,"[10] she begged him.

"Upon you be *what* iniquity, woman?" David's tone was belligerent.

"Please my lord, I saw not the young men you sent to Nabal, my husband. But see, I have provided. Please accept of my offering, that this shall be no grief unto thee."[11]

David surveyed the donkeys and their loads before turning back to Abigail. "You take the fool's sins on your own head?" inquired David. "You know the injustice and see us coming to right it, and now you beg for mercy upon thine house?"

"I beg for my house, yes, but for thee also, my lord, that

this shall not be an offence of heart unto thee, either that thou hast shed blood causeless, or that my lord hath avenged himself. For the Lord will certainly make thee a sure house because my lord fighteth the battles of the Lord, and evil hath not been found in thee all thy days. So it ever may be so, my lord, I pray thee, forgive the trespass of thine handmaid."[12]

David stood motionless, as if pondering a far-off thought that could be accessed only through still reflection. He looked deliberately at the provisions, thinking, and then down once more at Abigail. Slowly he released the hilt of his sword and dropped his hand to his side. She had yet to raise her eyes to his, but he looked tenderly upon her, his countenance soft. "Woman, what is your name?" His tone now was kind.

"Abigail, my lord."

"Rise, dear Abigail."

She arose to her knees, looking up at David.

"Who am I to withhold forgiveness from one such as you?" he said. "Blessed be the Lord God of Israel, which sent thee this day to meet me and which has kept me from striking you. And blessed be thine advice, and blessed be thou, dear Abigail, who hast kept me this day from sinning against the Lord. For as the Lord God of Israel liveth, if not for your intercession, by the morning I would have destroyed every male in thy household."[13]

"I accept of your offering," he continued. And then, to the

men behind him he shouted, "Elihu, Sidar, Gadriel, Joseph, come, gather the offering of the handmaiden of the Lord."

Four men hastened past David and began to transfer the goods from the donkeys.

Abigail fell again at David's feet. "Thank you, my lord. Blessed be thou and thy house."

David reached to her and pulled her to her feet. "Go up in peace to *thine* house, dear woman. See, I have hearkened to thy voice, and have accepted thy person. You have saved me from evil this day, which I will not forget."[14]

Abigail bowed her head slightly before him and then turned to leave. As she did so, her gaze met Rick's—startling him, as until then no one had seemed to notice his presence. Her gentle brown eyes shone brightly from above the veil that swept across her mouth. Her eyes reached to him more than any arms could have done—beckoning, inviting, and drawing him in. So kindly, they seemed windows into a deep pool of knowing, and when she looked upon him, Rick felt as much within her eyes as without.

He instantly felt as if they had had a conversation, or an interview, or, for that matter, a reunion. He perceived that she knew him—not just what could be understood by observing his person, but rather the *whole* of him—his past, his present, his future, his thoughts, his feelings, his fears. What's more, he felt that she treasured him, despite everything she knew. By the look in her eyes, Rick could tell she was smiling at him. After a few timeless seconds, she gently nodded, turned, and then continued up the path.

Rick, with David, stood transfixed, watching her disappear over the hill.

6

ATONEMENT

The spell, if that's what it was, was broken when Abigail passed from sight. Bewildered a bit by the experience, but still reveling in the warmth he had felt under her gaze, Rick turned to look at David. As he did so, he caught a glimpse of himself as well, just over David's left shoulder, about four rows back among the men. Rick could tell as he looked at himself and the other men that he and they were not pleased by the turn of events. Their faces showed disgust and frustration at turning back. It was evident that Abigail had not reached them as she had David.

David himself was a picture of peace and calm, his countenance purged of the anger that had darkened it since the report of Nabal's rebuff. As a man acquainted with war and with the mentality of those who wage it, he showed understanding as he mingled among his men, talking with and calming their spirits. Rick even thought he saw David's arm around his twin as they ambled away. Rick could see why the men followed David: he was one of them, which made them resonate with him, but he was beyond them as well, which made them reach.

"Amazing," Rick exclaimed to no one in particular, as the last man rounded the bend back toward Paran.

"Indeed," his grandfather nodded. "But why? What about this experience amazes you?"

"Well, didn't you see it?" Rick asked exuberantly, whirling to face his grandfather.

"Yes, I did. What I want to know is whether you did."

Rick returned a puzzled look.

"Tell me what you saw, Ricky."

"A miraculous end to a war that never began," he answered squarely, turning again toward Paran.

"Oh, but it had begun, Ricky, make no mistake. The war began when David and his men started seeking revenge in their hearts. The swinging of blades was a mere formality."

"Well, yes, I understand that. What I mean is—" but suddenly he couldn't find words to say. He had been struck by Abigail's actions, transfixed by her eyes, and had felt something powerful in his soul, but now as he tried to articulate the meaning of what he had witnessed he realized that he had mistaken the conviction he felt for understanding. *What _had_ just*

THE GIFT OF ABIGAIL

happened? He wasn't altogether sure. *But there was something about Abigail!*

"What I mean is," he continued, "Abigail made peace here. She changed David; I could see it in his eyes. And something about *her* eyes too—"

"What about them?"

"I don't know. She looked at me, and I felt something wonderful. I felt like she knew me, I mean really knew me—my background, my situation, my hopes, my struggles, everything. And it's funny to say, but in a way her eyes told me that she loved me, despite everything."

Grandpa Carson looked to the crest of the hill where they had last seen Abigail. "Do you know who she was, Ricky?"

"Yes, you told me yourself. She was the wife of Nabal."

"Yes. And who else?"

"Who *else?*" Rick repeated in surprise.

"Yes."

Rick stood pondering the question as his grandfather scrambled down the bank of the hill and onto the path. Rick followed him, and together they looked northward toward where Abigail had disappeared.

"Let me share something with you, Ricky. Walk with me." He started climbing the road toward Carmel, and Rick set off after him.

"Three days after the death of Christ," he began, "two believers walked the road to Emmaus, just as we are walking now, trying to make sense of the sudden and tragic end to their hopes and dreams. Jesus, their trusted Redeemer of Israel, was dead, his body gone. They wanted to believe the testimony of the women who said they had 'seen a vision of angels, which said that he was alive,'[15] but seemed to struggle at the thought. In their own words, they were 'astonished' by the story.

"They were confused and troubled, Ricky, as you might imagine. Events had failed to unfold as they had believed they must. 'How could the Redeemer of Israel die before Israel was redeemed?' they wondered aloud. Faith shaken, they struggled to find meaning in a tragedy that seemed to snatch all meaning from their lives.[16] Perhaps no road seemed longer than the road they were to walk that day.

"But like every long road we walk, these men did not walk it alone. The Redeemer they had hoped for not only lived, he was walking beside them. And he said to them, 'What manner of communications are these that ye have one to another, as ye walk, and are sad?'[17] After hearing their troubled response, the Lord made this key remark: 'O fools, and slow of heart to believe all that the prophets have spoken.' And then, beginning at Moses and through all the writings of the prophets, he taught them from all the scriptures 'the things concerning himself.'[18]

"In other words, Ricky, if the disciples had understood the scriptures, they wouldn't have been surprised by the events that troubled them. All of the scriptures testified of the Savior's life, suffering and death; they just hadn't seen how before.

"They were not alone in this, either. The remaining apostles were struggling with the same issues as they gathered in an upper room. The resurrected Lord appeared to them as well and said, 'Peace be unto you.'[19] But they were terrified, thinking he was a spirit. And then he told them, 'These are the words which I spake unto you, while I was yet with you, that all things must be fulfilled, which were written in the law of Moses, and in the prophets, and in the psalms, concerning me.'[20] Then, Ricky, he opened their understanding,[21] just as he had opened the understanding of the disciples on the road to Emmaus. He showed them how everything about his life and death was revealed in detail in the scriptures at a level that would survive the loss of plain and precious things—not only through direct prophecy but also indirectly through types, shadows, metaphors, and allegories. The prophet Nephi, in the Book of Mormon, put it well when he said, 'All things which have been given of God from the beginning of the world, unto man, are the typifying of Christ.'[22]

"So, Ricky," he said, as he stopped and faced him, "what might this suggest about the story of Abigail?"

"You're saying she's a 'type' of Christ."

"I'm saying it's worth pondering whether she is. After all, David himself said that she came at the Lord's direction and acted on his behalf.

"I'd invite you to consider what you have witnessed here in Abigail," he continued. "You may discover things in her that remind you of the Lord. In fact, if she turns out to be a type of Christ, her story may illuminate and clarify things about the Savior that you've never really thought about before—beautiful things, cleansing implications, saving truths. That is what her story has done for me. She has illuminated for me an aspect of the atonement that has blessed my life ever since. I believe it may bless yours as well. That is why we have come."

Rick's experience with Abigail had already riveted his attention, but this comment sobered him as well. "Okay," he began deliberately, "so you'd like me to think about Abigail and Christ—or rather, about how Abigail points to, or is a type of Christ."

Rick thought he noticed a slight nod, which he took to be assent, so he continued. "Well, let's see." His mind whirled back over what he had just witnessed. "Yes, I think I see what you mean. Abigail brought to David everything he needed—bread, wine, sheep, and so on—just like Jesus does for us, who is himself the bread of life, the true vine, and the lamb of God."

"Yes, Ricky. Good. That's an excellent insight."

"So in that respect Abigail is a 'type' of Christ," Rick continued, mostly to himself, feeling comfortable with his discovery. "I see it."

"Okay. But do you understand what difference it makes?"

"What do you mean?"

"It is one thing to notice what might be a type of the Savior and quite another to understand its purpose and meaning. So

Abigail supplied David with everything he had asked for and more—so what? What's the practical relevance? What's the point?"

"Does it have to have another point?" Rick asked, his confidence still strong. "I mean, here we have a story where the central peacemaking figure acts in similitude of the Savior. That strikes me as pretty significant."

"Yes, Ricky, but if you're willing to settle merely for that intellectual insight, then you will miss nearly everything Abigail has to offer. You have to ask more of the story than that. You have to dig into it, replay it, ponder it, savor it. If the story reveals something about peacemaking, as you say it does, but you yourself have not been brought closer to peace because of it, then either it is a trifling story or you haven't yet penetrated it—or allowed it to penetrate you. Don't be so quick to understand."

"Okay," Rick said, pensively, "then what am I missing?"

"Are you willing to look for it?"

"Yes."

"Then look."

"At what?"

"At what you have already seen. The story is rich, Ricky. Here David was, armed for battle, resolved to wipe out an entire estate and household, and a moment later he wished peace for the household and sent the family's matriarch and her servants away with his blessing. How did it happen, and what does it mean for us? Dig into the story, Ricky. As I said before, replay it in your mind—ponder it, savor it. Put yourself in it, which should be doubly interesting in this case since it seems you already *are* in it! What did Abigail say? What did she do? What did or didn't change in David? What did or didn't change in his men? Don't just watch, Ricky, search and *learn*."

"Okay," Rick said, beginning to feel a little perturbed. "As I said, the first thing Abigail did was bring to David the provisions Nabal had denied him. And you want me to get inside of that, to understand its relevance."

"I think that would be helpful, yes."

Then why don't you just tell me what you want me to say? he thought to himself. *Don't make me guess your thoughts.*

"I'm not interested in your guessing my thoughts, Ricky. I'm interested in your discovering your own."

Rick was stunned. "You can read my thoughts?"

"Sometimes. When the stakes are high."

"And the stakes are high now?"

"As high as they can get."

This sobered Rick immediately, and he began working anew on his grandfather's question as they walked.

"Maybe an analogy would help," his grandfather said, rescuing them both from the silence. "I remember how you loved baseball, Ricky. In fact, I still remember attending your games. You were a gifted shortstop."

Rick smiled at the compliment.

"We had some great times at those games, your family and I," Grandpa added. "Remember the state championship game your senior year?"

How could he forget? His team led by one run in the top of the final inning. Runners were on second and third with two outs when Rick committed an error that nearly cost them the game. On a routine ball to him that should have been the final out, he threw over the first baseman's head and the runners scored. If not for a miraculous two-run home run in the bottom of the inning by his teammate, Jason Taylor, to this day Rick would have been the goat in his hometown. As it was, most people had forgotten his error.

"Yes, I remember."

"I bet you started to offer up some mighty prayers after your error on that play—right out there on the field *and* in the dugout at the bottom of the inning. Am I right?"

Rick remembered both his embarrassment and his hope for a miracle rally. At first he had been too embarrassed to feel anything but shame, but as the inning closed with his team behind and their crowd anxious, Rick remembered hoping beyond hope that a teammate would make up for his error and win them the game. "That's true. When Jason hit that home run, it was the sweetest feeling. It was probably all the sweeter to me because of what he saved me from—not just a loss but also from a personal but very public failure. I felt redeemed, to tell you the truth."

"That's why I chose the story, Ricky. It's redemption that I'm interested in, and this story, combined with Abigail's, illuminates the atonement that makes redemption possible."

"How so?"

"Well, you're saying that your error put the team in a hole—not just you, but all your teammates as well, and also your fans, for that matter. Your error would result in a stinging loss for the team unless someone could do something to make up for it."

"Yes, I guess that's right, although I'd prefer if you would downplay the pain part a bit," Rick offered, only half in jest.

Grandpa Carson smiled. "Now think about the Abigail situation—"

"I get it," Rick interjected. "You're saying that Nabal and I each created a difficulty for others that someone else had to make up for, and that in that respect our stories are similar."

"Yes. Both you and Nabal increased the burdens and hardships of others, and in both cases, someone atoned for the wrongs of another—Jason in your case, and Abigail in Nabal's."

"Okay, I understand that."

"Do you?"

"Yes, I think so," Rick answered matter-of-factly.

"Then tell me what this reveals about the atonement."

"Well, it illustrates how Christ paid for our sins—that's what the atonement is about."

"So tell me then, Ricky, whose sins did Abigail atone for?"

"Nabal's, of course."

"Is that what the story reveals? Is it Nabal who is redeemed in Abigail's story?"

The question stumped Rick, and he puzzled over it. On the one hand, the story was clearly about an atonement for Nabal's sins—*wasn't it?* Yet just as clearly, Abigail came to David, not Nabal, so perhaps it was an atonement for David. *Wait a minute, that's not right,* Rick countered within. *Abigail came to David in order to save Nabal. Nabal was the one who was saved here, for if it hadn't been for Abigail's atonement, David would have wiped him out.*

"Yes, Nabal was definitely the person who was saved in this story."

Grandpa Carson looked oddly unconvinced. "Let's think about it a little more carefully," he said. "If the atonement is for the redemption of sins to save the sinner, in order to understand who is redeemed in this story, perhaps we should first be clear on the identity of the sinner."

"That's easy: Nabal. Nabal is the sinner and David is the sinned-against, the aggrieved party, the victim."

"Are you sure about that?" his grandfather questioned. "I rather think this is primarily a story about *David's* sin and redemption, not Nabal's."

"*David's* sin? Why not Nabal's? What did David do?"

Grandpa Carson took a long look at Rick. "Remember when I told you about Uncle Joe?"

"Yes."

"And remember how you kept insisting that I had done nothing wrong, that Joe was the one with the problem—the 'sinner,' in a sense?"

"Sure. And I still actually think that. Although I suppose you did play a part in the fourteen-year period of silence," he allowed.

"But you're only thinking about our actions, Ricky. What about our *hearts*? Remember the Pharisees—they of the perfect actions. Their hearts were corrupt and the Savior branded them as the vilest sinners of the day, notwithstanding their outwardly righteous acts. We sin when our hearts are sinful, no matter what we do on the surface. The law and the prophets hang on the two great commandments of loving God and others because if our hearts fail to love, neither the law nor the prophets, nor anything else—including outward 'righteousness'—can save us.

"So 'what did David do?' you ask—what was his sin? He carried a sinful heart, my boy, a heart that burned with envy and rage, a heart that had turned from the Spirit. Unless and until he was redeemed from that sinfulness, he would never taste eternal life."

"Okay, but what about *Nabal?*" Rick blurted, thinking about Carol while he said it. "Didn't he carry the same kind of heart?"

"Yes, it certainly appears that he did, Ricky," Grandpa

Carson responded, measuring Rick for a moment. "So the story of Abigail is not merely the story of a single sinner, is it? It is rather the story of David responding sinfully to the sin of another."

This satisfied Rick for the moment.

"You have learned since you were young that the atonement was for the sinner," his grandfather continued, "and that certainly is true, but it is only half the story, and the second half is not nearly so well understood. The story of Abigail suggests that the atonement is as much for the benefit of the sinned against—the victim of sin—as for the sinner. But her story goes beyond even that. It suggests also that one of the effects of sin is to invite those who have been sinned against—David, in this case—to become sinful themselves, and that the atonement provides the escape from such provocation to sin. This is David's story here. What Abigail provided for David was a way of escape from his sin of sinning against a sinner!" Grandpa Carson paused for a moment to give time for those thoughts to settle.

"When Abigail knelt before David with all that he needed," he continued, "her purpose was to redeem David from *his* sin. Perhaps she would later kneel before Nabal and offer a similar redemption." After a brief pause, he continued. "Now when—"

"Wait, Grandpa," Rick interrupted. "I want to make sure I understand what you are saying. Walk me through this again— what you've just been explaining."

"Sure. What I said was that when people think of the atonement, they most often think about how the Savior filled in the gaps for their *own* sins, which he surely did. That is, we are all sinners, and someone had to bridge for each of us the otherwise impassible chasm between us and eternal life that we have created through sin. So normally we think of the atonement as something that Christ has done for *us*—for *ourselves*. But Abigail invites us to look at the atonement from a different angle—not from the perspective of how Christ has atoned for our *own* sins, but rather from the equally true perspective that he has atoned for the sins of *others*. And part of that atonement, Abigail suggests, is the idea that the Lord offers to those who have been harmed or potentially harmed by the sins of others the help and sustenance they need to be made whole. Those deprived of love can receive *his* love. The companionless can find a companion in *him*. Those with a cross to bear can find another who carries and makes it light. With their burdens lifted in this way, the sinned-against are saved from the provocation to sin and are therefore redeemed from their *own* sins."

Grandpa Carson paused. "Does that make sense to you, Ricky?"

In truth, Rick was struggling. He understood the ideas with his mind, but his heart was lagging behind, fighting the implications. It was comfortable and clear to equate Carol to sinful Nabal, for example, and himself to a righteous David. He could now begin to think about David as being sinful, but he couldn't get past the thought that Nabal was worse and that somehow that should matter. He wasn't perfect, he was willing to admit that, but Carol was far worse. And given that, he didn't see how he could be expected to be much better than he was. He also hadn't felt much, if any, of the atoning help his grandpa was talking about, and it seemed to him that if anyone deserved it, he did. "I see your logic, Grandpa," Rick said after a few moments. "But I'm still trying to understand it. I'm not entirely sure what it means yet, practically speaking."

At that, Rick paused for a moment to collect his thoughts. But they resisted collection. "Do you believe what you're saying, Grandpa?" he asked finally. "I mean, *really?* Do you believe that the Lord offers the kind of help you're talking about to those who have been hurt? Has he given it to *you?*"

Grandpa slowed to a stop. "Do you remember Joseph in Egypt, Ricky? Have you ever marveled at how he was able to receive his brothers so graciously after what they had done to him?[23] Or Daniel, and Meshach, Shadrach, and Abed-nego, who were strengthened by the Lord in the trials they suffered at the hands of others?[24] Or the people of Alma in the Book of Mormon whose heavy burdens at the hands of the Lamanites were made light so that they 'could not feel them upon their backs'?[25] Or David, here, whose own hardships because of others' sins were atoned for and eased and who, as a result, was able to love Saul all his days even though Saul never stopped trying to kill him?[26] Yes. I believe it, Ricky, and I've felt this help many times myself. The Lord packs for each of us, as it were, living bread, water, sheep, corn, raisins, and figs, and comes to us with that offering, inviting us to accept of his atonement for others' sins. And when we do, as David, Alma, Joseph, Daniel, Meshach, Shadrach, or Abed-nego did, we find ourselves blessed with all that is needful, and we also find that we are cleansed from sinfulness ourselves.

"So, yes, Ricky, I believe it. In fact, my knowledge is sure concerning it. My question is, will *you* believe it?"

7

FORGIVENESS

Grandpa Carson looked solemnly at Rick before resuming his walk. Rick was a little slower to join him this time but was back at his side within a minute or so.

"I want to believe, Grandpa. I really do. But let me tell you what I am struggling with. If what you say is true, then the Lord presumably would strengthen me in my struggles with Carol. His atonement for her sins would include making up for the burdens those sins are placing upon me, or at the very least would include the blessing of having those burdens made light. That's what you are saying, right?"

His grandfather didn't respond.

"But that hasn't been my experience," Rick continued. "I don't feel the help you say the Lord is offering. In fact, I've never felt so alone or deprived in my life—just at the time when

I need his help the most. If anything, the burdens I feel are only becoming heavier. So if the Lord is before me, as Abigail, offering to supply what I am lacking, he sure is being quiet. I don't hear a thing."

The words shocked Rick when he heard himself say them. He had heard such bitterness from others' lips, but had always pitied the complainers for their lack of faith. The thought made him feel all the more hopeless.

His grandfather continued walking in silence. They had by now passed the crest of the initial hill and had reached the top of a smaller hill farther on. As the ground started to level, a host of additional hills rose before them. The road they were walking meandered its way between and up these hills before it disappeared a few miles in the distance. Grandpa Carson stopped and turned to look back at the path they had climbed.

"Ricky, let me ask you something. You saw Abigail and the effect she had on David."

"Yes," Rick answered pensively.

"Do you suppose that her offering had the same effect on David's men as it did on him?"

Rick remembered the frustration he witnessed in many of the men—his own twin included—when David informed them that they would be returning without a fight. David had had to cajole and comfort them in order to calm their spirits.

"No," Rick answered. "Most of the men weren't very happy."

"That's right. And they weren't happy even though Abigail

had been kneeling before them as well as before David. They never recognized her offering for what it was. In a way, they didn't even see her, even though she was right before them."

"Is that what you think I'm doing?" Rick asked directly. "Are you saying that the Lord is right before me just as Abigail was before those men, but that I, like them, am failing to see it?"

"Well, Ricky, you were in that group of men. *Did* you see it?"

Rick felt as if he had been punched in the stomach. The comment stunned him, like he had been the victim of a most unexpected and devastating checkmate. He stood still, trying to comprehend the implications of his grandfather's comment. *I was in the group, as he said,* he thought. *And he's right; Abigail didn't reach me. I didn't recognize her for who she was. Why, Lord?* he finally cried. *If you are there, Lord, why can't I hear you? What have I done to turn you away?*

"He never turns away, Ricky." His grandfather was reading his thoughts again. "And it isn't so much what you have done as what you haven't done."

"Then what *haven't* I done?"

"The answer you seek is revealed in what you have witnessed today. Although the Lord stands before us offering the help we need, there is a condition we must meet in order to see and receive of his atonement offering. David met that condition; many of his men—you included—did not. If you want the

Lord's atonement to work in your behalf, Ricky, you must meet this condition yourself."

"So what is it?" Rick begged.

"Something you must discover for yourself."

At that, Grandpa Carson turned back in the direction of Carmel and resumed walking.

Rick walked silently beside him. *A condition in the story of Abigail,* he kept repeating to himself as they walked. *Something that must be met in order to recognize and accept her offering.* Rick could see nothing. *What condition did David meet that his men did not?* Abigail herself placed no conditions on anyone in the story that Rick could see. She simply made her offering. The only condition was whether or not David and his men would accept it. *But that isn't what Grandpa was talking about,* he thought to himself. *There is something in the story that is a key to whether they will accept it in the first place.*

"I can't think of anything," Rick finally said in frustration. "I don't see any conditions in the story other than the question of whether those before whom Abigail bowed would accept her offering."

"Think a little harder, Ricky. Think about what Abigail *did* in the story. She did more than offer a load of provisions. She did at least two other things that are critical and extraordinary—two additional things that are types and shadows of what Christ himself did. When you discover those two acts, you will discover as well the condition upon which Abigail's, and the Savior's, atonement is predicated."

Two other things that Abigail did. Rick went to work on the problem the way he sometimes did the *New York Times* crossword puzzle. *Let's replay what she did,* he thought. *She rode down the hill, her servants and the provisions before her. Okay, and then she got off her donkey when she saw David and his men and rushed forward and bowed herself to the earth. Okay, these were two things she did, but are they important? Do these reveal the condition Grandpa is talking about? Do they point to Christ? I don't see it. Then David approached her, and she fell at his feet. And then what happened? Let's see, she said something to him. Yes, she said something like, 'On me be the sin.' That's it! She took Nabal's sin on her own head, and in that act she resembled the Savior.*

"Grandpa, she took Nabal's sin on her own head."

Grandpa Carson smiled and stopped. "Yes, Ricky, that's right. She pleaded with David, 'Upon me let this iniquity be.'[27] Well done. But do you know what it means?"

"Sure, it was her way of begging David to forgive Nabal and let go of his anger."

"It seems that way, doesn't it?"

"Yes, it does. You're saying that that's *wrong?*" Rick didn't see how it could be wrong.

Grandpa Carson smiled slightly and set off again.

"Is that wrong, Grandpa?" Rick asked again as he drew to his side. "If so, *how?* I want to see."

"There is a final thing that Abigail did in similitude of Christ that will answer your question, Ricky—a final, astonishing act that illuminates what it means to have taken another's sins on one's own head. See that and you will discover the understanding you seek."

What else did Abigail do that points to Christ? Rick was searching seriously now. *She pleaded with him not to do what he was about to do. Maybe that's it,* he thought. *I can imagine that Christ pleads that way with us. Yes, that's precisely what the Spirit does all the time—invites us to do certain things and pleads with us to avoid others. But is that an astonishing thing, as Grandpa said? Does that illuminate the meaning of taking sins on one's head?* Rick couldn't see how. *Maybe I'm missing something else,* he thought. *What else did she do?*

"Grandpa, I don't see anything—at least nothing we haven't talked about already. Unless you're referring to the way Abigail pleaded with David not to do what he was about to do."

"That's part of it, Ricky. But there was something she did, or rather said, that made her pleading efficacious."

Something she said. What else did she say? Rick tried to remember everything he had heard but nothing leaped out at him—certainly nothing "astonishing," as his grandfather had described this final act to be.

Grandpa Carson stopped walking and turned to Rick, who couldn't help but notice what wonderful shape his grandfather seemed to be in. He wasn't even sweating, while Rick himself was beginning to pay dearly for the heat. "You're thinking hard about it, Ricky, I appreciate that. You deserve another look."

At this, Rick's mind was swept back in memory. He was standing once more on the rock overlooking the path. Abigail was at David's feet.

> "Upon me, my lord, upon me let this iniquity be."
>
> "Upon you be <u>what</u> iniquity, woman?"
>
> "Please my lord, I saw not the young men you sent to Nabal, my husband. But see, I have provided. Please accept of my offering, that this shall be no grief unto thee."
>
> "You take the fool's sins on your own head? You know the injustice and see us coming to right it, and now you beg for mercy upon thine house?"
>
> "I beg for my house, yes, but for thee also, my lord, that this shall not be an offence of heart unto thee, either that thou hast shed blood causeless, or that my lord hath avenged himself. For the Lord will certainly make thee a sure house because my lord fighteth the battles of the Lord, and evil hath not been found in thee all thy days. So it ever may be so, my lord, I pray thee, forgive the trespass of thine handmaid."[28]

"Forgive the trespass of thine handmaid!"[29] The words gripped Rick's mind.

"Grandpa!" Rick exclaimed, the path and his grandfather reconstructing themselves before Rick's eyes as he said it. "She said, 'Forgive the trespass of thine handmaid.' That's what you're talking about, isn't it? That's the astonishing act you are referring to."

"Yes, Ricky, it is. And why is it so astonishing?"

"Because she hadn't done anything wrong!" Rick answered excitedly, his heart racing with the discovery. "She had committed no trespass. And yet she begged David to forgive her all the same—not Nabal, but *her,* as if *she* were the one who had done the wrong. She didn't say, 'Please forgive Nabal his trespass,' which she could have said. She said rather, 'Forgive the trespass of thine handmaid'—'forgive *my* trespass.' She claimed the sin as her own. Which implies," he continued, his mind racing with interest but also now with a bit of confusion, "that Christ did the same—that having taken upon himself the sins of those who have wronged us, Christ now comes to us and asks us to forgive *him* the trespass." He paused to consider this.

"Is that right?" he asked, struggling with the implications if it was. "No, it can't be!" he exclaimed, answering his own question. "The Savior never did anything wrong. He's sinless. He doesn't need us to forgive him!"

"No, Ricky, he certainly doesn't," Grandpa Carson agreed.

"Then I'm not sure I know what you're saying."

Grandpa Carson breathed in deeply, the way one does in the moment he realizes that greater patience and deliberation is needed. He looked pleasantly at Rick. "You're right, Ricky. The Lord doesn't need forgiveness at all. The act of taking others' sins upon himself did not make him sinful. In fact, as you just witnessed with Abigail, willingness to assume another's sins is actually an expression of sinlessness.

"However, this aspect of the story of Abigail—namely, that one who didn't need forgiveness nevertheless asked for it—illuminates something very important about forgiveness. It illustrates who forgiveness is for."

"'Who forgiveness is for'?"

"Yes."

"I guess I'm not exactly sure what you mean."

"Abigail did not need to be forgiven for anything, and yet still she asked," his grandfather replied. "So when she asked David for forgiveness, she wasn't asking because she needed to be forgiven. There was another reason for her plea."

Rick wondered at this for a moment. "Okay, what *was* it?" he asked, when nothing came to mind. "What was the reason?"

"Do you remember the scripture where the Lord says, 'I, the Lord, will forgive whom I will forgive, but of you it is required to forgive all men'?"[30]

"Yes."

"That is your answer, Ricky. Abigail asked for forgiveness not because *she* needed to be forgiven but because David needed to forgive."

Rick's mind was swimming. "That doesn't seem right, Grandpa. I mean, didn't Abigail need David to forgive her? After all, he was on his way to destroy her house."

"Yes, but remember her words to him: 'That this shall be no grief unto thee,' she said, 'nor offence of heart unto my lord.'[31]

"Abigail's message was that forgiveness was for the one who was forgiving, not the one who was being forgiven. David needed to forgive so that, in the words of Abigail, 'he would continue to be found without evil, so that the Lord could make him a sure house.'[32] David might have felt justified in withholding this forgiveness from Nabal, however sinful such withholding might have been, but from Abigail? No, her offering on behalf of another obliterated every justification David might otherwise have had. She freed him from the blind comfort of his grudges. Through this merciful act, she created for David the most forgiveness-friendly environment that could possibly be created. David was never more able to do what he needed most to do—forgive, or more precisely, repent of his failing to forgive—than when the request for forgiveness was made by one who had atoned in full for the sin David was raging against.

"The Lord, by taking the sins of our Nabals upon his head, extends us the same mercy. 'Upon me let this iniquity be,' he pleads. 'Let me deal with it if there is any dealing to be done. But you, my dear son or dear daughter, let it go. Let me take it, as I already have done. Forgive.'

"Although the Lord doesn't actually ask us to forgive *him*, the effect of the atonement is such that it's *as if* that is what he is asking. 'Inasmuch as ye have done it [or done it not] unto one of the least of these,' the Savior taught, 'ye have done it [or done it not] unto me.'[33] When we withhold forgiveness from others," Grandpa continued, "we are in effect saying that the atonement alone was insufficient to pay for this sin. We are holding out for more. We are finding fault with the Lord's offering. We are in essence demanding that the Lord repent of an insufficient atonement. So when we fail to forgive another, it is as if we are failing to forgive the Lord—who, as you already rightly said, needs no forgiveness."

Rick looked away from his grandfather, and his eyes and countenance fell toward the ground. "I wish you could teach this to Carol," he said despairingly, heaving a heavy sigh.

"Is that what you think you need, Ricky—for *Carol* to know this? That your problems would be solved if *she* got better at repenting?"

Rick was battling himself. His mind heard the irony in his grandfather's question, but his heart silently nodded in consent.

"Whether Carol needs this understanding or not really isn't the issue for you, is it, Ricky? What you need is not *her* repentance but your own. That is, what you need is not *her* forgiveness *of you*, but rather, *your* forgiveness *of her*. You must repent of your own sin of failing to forgive. That is the understanding Abigail offers. You believe you are withholding something Carol needs when you are withholding forgiveness from her, but there is nothing further from the truth. Through the crucible of the atonement, the Lord has already forged forgiveness for her. What more could *your* forgiveness add? No, Carol doesn't need you to forgive her. *You* need you to forgive her, Ricky. So the Lord in his mercy comes to you and says, 'The atonement applies as much to Carol as it does to you, my son. I have claimed her sins and taken them upon me. Let it go.'

"You should consider," he continued, "how your failure to forgive is in effect a withholding from the Lord—he who has claimed and atoned for the sins and weaknesses in Carol that you insist on carrying with a grudge."

This comment hit Rick like a blow to the head. This was no longer just a lesson about the atonement. It was rather an indictment of his life, and it left Rick speechless. The idea that *he* was fundamentally in the wrong thrust him deep into the pain of his troubles. He found himself transported in memory to three mornings before.

Carol was in tears that morning and reported through her sobs, as she often did, that she was feeling overwhelmed. She had been feeling ill and had been complaining that a pending assignment with the PTA was weighing her down, but Rick knew her complaint was only so much smoke. She could make a mountain out of any molehill. She became overwhelmed so often, and over the smallest things, that Rick had finally concluded that she *needed* to feel overwhelmed. For some deep, dark, sick reason, she *had* to feel bad and depressed and no good. It relieved her of responsibility, and Rick was sick of it.

He provided her with an ideal life, as he saw it. He made an ample enough living to allow her to stay home in comfort, and he made no demands of her whatsoever. He worked, sure, but he also took care of the kids most of the moments he was home and did whatever else he could find the energy to do around the house, but it was never enough.

So when Carol had said—again—that she was feeling overwhelmed, Rick took it as thinly veiled code for "You aren't doing enough for me," and silently, his whole soul threw up its arms in disgust. *How could I do any more than I'm already doing?* he cried within. *What about _me_ being overwhelmed? Maybe I should start complaining about all _my_ burdens so I can start claiming victimhood _myself_! It's a pretty overwhelming thing to be living with you, you know.* But he didn't say this, at least not verbally, and his relative forbearance added to his feeling of moral superiority. "You're not the only one with a lot to do, you know," he had allowed himself to bark before turning his back and walking briskly out the door.

He had replayed that scene over and over in his mind all day at work, adding it to his increasingly unbearable collection of grievances. He dreaded going home, and when he finally did, he could not bring himself to look at Carol. She too was stiff and silent, and the air between them crackled. They passed each other in silence all night long, awkwardly looking away or burying themselves in the kids or the paper or the dishes—anything to escape a conversation.

Carol climbed the stairs to the bedroom about 10:00 P.M., early by about an hour, and Rick heaved a sigh of relief. He plopped heavily on the couch to decompress in front of the TV. He went to bed at about 12:30 A.M.

He and Carol had not spoken from that day to this, and the wintry silence had only grown colder.

What did Abigail have to do with this? he puzzled within. *What am I missing? Lord, if I am missing something here, help me to see what I am missing.*

In the silence that followed, Rick could feel a voice—and feel is the right word because he didn't perceive it with his ears. It was rather a kind of still whisper in his chest that reached toward his heart and beckoned him to some inner region where love still flowered and hope still bloomed. For a moment Rick gave up the bitter monologue about Carol that had been occupying his mind and tuned himself toward the voice. As he did so the pain he had been feeling dissipated, only to be replaced just as quickly with a different pain—a pain at once similar and yet completely different. He was feeling Carol's pain, and he perceived her lying on the bed beside him even while he stood with his grandfather on the road to Carmel. Her pain was as great as his own. He recognized the dashed hopes, the loneliness, the feelings of abandonment and betrayal. He felt her concern for the children, her grief over the loss of her spouse's love, her fear of an uncertain future. Rick was overcome and fell to the ground.

His grandfather knelt beside him, and began brushing Rick's cheek with his hand.

As he lay there, Rick lost hold of the image of his sleeping wife and began to feel the burden of one who must live with a person in such pain. The love and hope he had felt for a moment were disappearing under the weight of self-pity.

"My son," Grandpa said gently, "when the Savior comes to you with the sins of others upon him, he offers you a view of others that only he knows. He begs you to see as he sees—as One who knows every pain, insecurity, aspiration, and infirmity because he has taken them upon himself. He will show you others as *he* sees and loves them, and he will help you to see and love them that way as well, for he begs you not merely to ungird your sword but to ungird your heart. If you do, the miracle of his atonement will flow freely, and you, like David, will put down war and take up bread and drink and sheep and figs."

"I saw something for a moment, Grandpa," Rick whispered. "For a moment I understood what you have been saying. But the clarity is already fading. I'm not sure I can do what you're suggesting. I'm not sure I can let it go." Rick was near despair and fighting back tears.

They sat together for a moment in silence. Grandpa Carson turned to look at the hills that lay before them. "You don't need to let it go, Ricky. It will go by itself if you remember Abigail and come to the Lord. He has already let it go for you. That is part of his atonement. You just need to allow him to take it from you."

With this, he began to stand up. "I leave you with three things to remember, my son. First, thinking of Abigail, remember that the Lord has taken the sins of others on his own head. Second, remember that he has atoned for those sins and that our failure to forgive is therefore in essence a withholding from the Lord. And finally, remember that if we grant this forgiveness in full, he atones in full for the pain and burdens that have come at others' hands. He blesses us with his own love, his own appreciation, his own companionship, his own strength to endure. And if we have these, what do we lack?"

With that, he set off again toward Carmel.

"Wait, Grandpa, wait!" Rick yelled as he scrambled to his feet.

But his grandfather was moving at an incredible speed.

"I must go now, my boy," he called. "Perhaps I will be able to visit you again. I would like that."

"So would I," Rick called after him, tears cutting paths down his dusty cheeks.

PART II

THE IMPLICATION OF NINEVEH

8

THE STORM CONTINUES

D addy, I want a drink of water."
Rick cleared his bleary eyes and saw a tussle of hair. It was Lauren, her little head just high enough to peer over the side of the bed. Like clockwork, here she was again at 2:00 A.M. Rick could count on one hand the uninterrupted nights of sleep he'd had over the last few months. Lauren was addicted to middle-of-the-night drinks, and the full glass of water Rick placed on her nightstand every night apparently tasted much better if Daddy got out of bed to give it to her.

Rick sometimes resented that he was the one who was always up with the kids, and this night was no different. But as Lauren took her drink, pointed her cheek at him for a kiss, and then said, as she always did, "I love you, Daddy," as he walked away, he was grateful for the mop-headed interruption.

Rick could usually quickly resume his dreaming, but tonight sleep eluded him. Thoughts of David, Abigail, the road to Carmel, and his grandpa whirled through his mind. Rick remembered the example of a Church-member friend who had told him that he slept with a tablet of paper by his bed so he could record whatever was on his mind in the early morning moments when he awoke. This brother claimed he had discovered some of the most poignant counsel of his life on that tablet come morning time. This thought too began to nag at him, keeping him awake, but he knew of no paper nearby, and the cold night shoved him further under the covers.

Rick lay thinking about what he had just witnessed. The visit with his grandfather remained as tactile and real as any real-life memory. He could still almost feel the desert breeze. And he remembered David and Abigail down to the threads of their robes. Although the dream, with its details, remained vividly with him, he struggled mightily with its implications.

Carol lay next to him, still facing away and hugging her side of the bed as she had been a few hours earlier. His grandfather's message echoed within him. *Remember three things,* he had said. *First, Christ took upon his own head the sins of those who have wronged us. Second, because of this, he stands between us and those whom we think have wronged us, asking us to realize that the atonement is sufficient for those sins and to therefore repent of our grudges and give up our enmity. And finally, if we forgive, the*

*atonement fills us with what we have lacked and either washes away
our pain, or sustains us in it.*

The memory of that counsel softened Rick a little more,
and as he looked at Carol, he felt a tinge of regret for his part
in the events that had pushed her to the far side of the bed. As
he looked upon her sleeping form, he wished for her to be back
in the center, where she used to sleep, and reached timidly to
rest his hand against her back. *Strange,* he thought to himself,
*how someone married for twelve years could feel as awkward touch-
ing his spouse as he did the first time he held her hand.* As he lay
pondering this, "tragic" seemed a more appropriate word.

So you hurt like I hurt, he thought, remembering the
moment in his dream. *The cold I have felt from you is your desperate attempt to freeze out the pain of failed expectations and the
humiliation of spousal rejection.* He was cold in just the same
way, and for the same reasons.

He had often complained to himself that Carol made herself as difficult to love as she could and then held it against him
when he did not love her fully. But he had a new sense that he
might perhaps be doing something similar to her. They were
locked in a kind of death spiral—an insane game of chicken
where each of them found themselves barreling toward an
unthinkable end, each so committed to the justice of their own
course that they were refusing to turn until too late.

Why would we do that? he wondered. *What's the point? Why
are we so willing, even driven, to risk everything?* He didn't have

a clue, and although he was feeling tinges of regret, he was filled more than ever with despair.

So what are we going to do? He asked himself, now turning to his back and looking at the ceiling. *How can we get out of the mess we're in? How is it possible?*

Why would it be impossible? came another thought.

This new idea was so unlike his normal despairing thoughts of late that he reflexively looked around the room to see if someone was there. Finding no one, he turned his eyes back to the ceiling.

Okay, he thought, turning the question into a challenge, *why would it be impossible?* But he couldn't fully take the bait, for the second voice within him kept insisting that healing *was* possible. Notwithstanding this, however, the first voice didn't believe it would happen. He, or Carol, or both, wouldn't be able to do what was needed, it told him. And the first voice was winning the argument.

If it is possible but you don't believe it will happen, then you don't really want it to happen, came the second voice. *There is something you want more than healing.*

What would I want more than healing! Rick retorted, joining the internal battle.

Unhappiness, pain, despair.

That's absurd!

Is it?

Why would I want to be unhappy, in pain, or despairing?

Good question. Why do you?

I don't!

Then why are you?

Because—well, because Carol makes happiness impossible! he exploded, adding an angry, unspoken expletive.

Rick had recently begun swearing internally, although the habit had not yet reached his lips. That one who knew better would be driven to profanity was to Rick just additional evidence of Carol's downward influence.

Sure, she seems fine now while she's sleeping, he defended himself. *And I might be able to imagine things being better between us. But I know what she'll be like come morning. And I don't deserve it! I don't deserve what she does to me!*

So you want what you deserve, do you? came the second voice.

Yes. That's all I'm asking, answered Rick.

"Are you sure you'd be willing to live with that?"

But this voice didn't come from within.

9

THE CAUSE OF THE STORM

Rick's hair was blowing in a stiff breeze. He looked to be in the middle of a sea or ocean, on the deck of an old-world wooden ship, about sixty feet in length. The wind was blowing briskly from the direction of a churning yellow sky as deckhands raced to and fro securing ropes and adjusting riggings. His grandfather was standing beside him.

Rick surveyed the scene. The vessel looked to be about twenty feet across for most of its length before rounding gently toward the bow and stern. From each end rose identical stem posts about ten feet in height, jutting from the tips of the ship toward the sky in arches like the forward end of ice-skating blades. A single mast towered midway on the deck, on which a large rectangular sail, quilted for strength with leather belts, was bursting with wind. The sky was darkening by the second.

Raindrops from the leading edge of the storm were just reaching the deck, and the sea began to kick at the hull. Rick looked skeptically at the crates and barrels that were stacked two deep along the edges of the deck. Expertly tied ropes appeared to hold them securely against the ship's sides, helped marginally by a wicker fence that ran the length of the ship. *But would they hold under the fury of the coming storm?* Rick wasn't so sure. Neither, apparently, were the mariners, for they were checking and rechecking every knot.

"Where are we, Grandpa?" Rick shouted above the gathering gale. The wind seemed to sweep his words out to sea.

"On a ship bound for Tarshish," his grandfather called back.

"Pardon me?"

"Tarshish," he yelled louder. "A town in the southwest of what *we* know as Spain—in *this* day the westernmost point of the known world."

"Why?" Rick called. "Why are we here?"

His grandfather motioned him over to a large crate that shielded them from the brunt of the wind.

They pressed themselves against the crate and huddled close together so they could speak and hear more clearly. Just then, the boat pitched suddenly, as if it fell in a hole on the starboard side, and a wave hurled itself over the crate that was their protection. Rick clutched at the ropes, entangling his arms around them in an effort to strap himself in.

"What are we doing here?" he gasped.

"You wanted what you deserved." His grandfather replied with remarkable calm considering the circumstances.

"Huh?"

"Just a moment ago you said that Carol isn't treating you as you deserve to be treated. All you want is what you deserve. Right?"

"Well, yes, I guess that's right. But what does that have to do with being *here?*"

"Ah, you're not the only one asking that question tonight."

Rick had no idea what his grandfather was talking about.

Just then a booming voice could be heard above the tumult. "Oarsmen! To your posts! To your posts!" Men scurried by them and disappeared down a hatch at midship. A few scrambled to lower the sail.

By now most of the sky was a foreboding black. Where light still shone, the clouds churned and swirled in sinister yellows and reds. The heavens were alive and moving, like a slithering mass of snakes. The ship pitched violently as if on a massive roller coaster. Waves began to rise far above them and then crash down across the deck. On the third of these blows a barrel near the bow on the port side burst free, hurling itself through the wicker barrier and out to sea. The crates and barrels behind it started sliding all over the deck, crashing against the other cargo. When the ship pitched again, all of the loose items flew from the deck.

"Overboard!" cried the booming voice they had heard a couple of minutes earlier. "Throw the cargo overboard!"

The men who had been securing the sail quickly loosened the knots around the cargo and started heaving crates over the side. Others joined them from below. After about ten minutes and countless close calls of men almost being thrown in the sea, the deck had been cleared of most of the freight.

The mariners scrambled headlong down the hatch. Rick instinctively followed, his grandfather close behind. Halfway down the ladder the ship rolled entirely on its side, throwing Rick against the starboard side of the hold. The vessel groaned as it slowly righted itself.

If things had been crazy on deck, it was mayhem down below. Men were wailing in prayer in ankle-high water, their voices and faces desperate. Some had loosened their tunics and tied the ends to secure objects, making crude harnesses in an attempt to keep their bodies from hurtling across the hold. Others were clutching desperately to the arms, legs, or harnesses of their comrades, or else to the ropes of the crates that filled about a third of the area. The crates were wedged tightly together and for the moment, at least, appeared secure.

"Call to the gods!" came the booming voice once more. Rick whirled to his left and saw a sturdy, weather-beaten man, perhaps fifty years old or so, with sun-dried skin and meaty, heavy eyes stretched wide with concern. The men obliged, calling heavenward with even greater intensity. The man with the voice—surely the captain, Rick thought—looked quickly from here to there around the whole of the interior that was visible from the hold. Rick followed his eyes wherever they looked but noticed nothing remarkable—a seam here and a joint there. The captain walked around and between the men, steadying himself on their shoulders as he went, combing every inch of the hold with his purposeful eyes. Just then, the ship rolled nearly to its side, throwing the captain halfway across the space. Water poured in through cracks in the hatch. "Keep pleading!" he shouted again as he rose to his feet, the ship creaking loudly as it struggled to right itself. He then pounded on the ceiling on the port side of the hold. "Row harder!" he yelled, apparently to oarsmen in a chamber between the cargo hold and the deck. He pounded on the ceiling on the stern side and repeated his call, adding, "Take us to land! Take us to land!" He then disappeared beyond the crates to the back.

Rick's grandfather was leaning against the wall to Rick's right. He was a picture of calm.

"What's the point of all this, Grandpa?"

Just then a man to Rick's left cried out, "The gods are angry. Who has brought this upon us?" A few of the others responded in unison, "Yes, who?" The men began eyeing each other warily. The prayers stopped, and the chamber was suddenly awash in a flood of acrimony and accusation. "You despicable thief!" screamed a toothless man on the opposite side of the hold. "*You* are responsible!" He loosed himself from his harness and threw himself toward a lanky youngster in the middle of the hold. Others jumped in on either side of the conflict, and the space became a blur of fists.

Another pitch to the port side threw the mass of them together against the far wall with a loud thump, their wet garments splattering against the boards.

The men momentarily forgot their feud as they checked themselves for injury but seemed ready to resume the fight until one of them suggested casting lots to see who was responsible. "Yes, let's," agreed the others, eager to find an acceptable way out of the melee.

Rick watched curiously as the men spread into a circle. The captain, who had emerged from the back of the hold with another man, joined in the circle, as did his new companion. This second man was different from the rest of the men on the crew. He was dressed as David and his men had been, although more nicely, with a robe (which was wet all along the side and back, as if he had been lying in the water that now lined the hold), head covering, and sandals, whereas most of the mariners were barefoot and, besides their undergarments, wore only tunics, with linen bands around their heads like belts to secure their hair. The newcomer's eyes were clouded by a look of resignation. He took his place next to the captain in the circle.

"Tolar, get the men!" the captain commanded, motioning to the compartments above them. The young man who had been the object of the toothless man's fury leapt to his feet and knocked three times against the port-side ceiling. He then repeated the same knock on the starboard side. On each side of the hold, a hatch in the ceiling opened, and a half-dozen men dropped from each of them. Their tunics were pulled down to their waists, secured only by a belt. Beads of sea water and sweat streamed down their bare chests.

"Fall in the circle," said the captain.

When all had hastily seated themselves, the most elderly-looking mariner among them began to chant some kind of incantation, the sound and language of which was completely foreign to Rick. The chant was a ritual of prayer to the storm god of the Phoenicians, inhabitants of the area known in modern times as Lebanon, who from 1000 B.C. to 700 B.C. were lords of ship building and ancient commerce—rulers of the seas from the coast of Israel to the mouth of the Atlantic, and from there north and south to the English isles and West African coast, respectively.

"Get on with it!" growled the toothless man who had led the attack a minute before. The old man stopped the prayer and pulled a pouch from his belt, from which he drew a dozen or so tiny beads and showed them to the circle. Rick's eyes were drawn to a brilliant purple bead that stood out from the others.

"We need a dry surface; there is too much water on the floor," the man said.

The captain raised himself with a loud grunt, walked back

to the cargo, and with nothing but his bare hands ripped the lid off a large crate. He dragged it back to the circle and flung it in the middle of the men. "There, get on with it, Rabish," he said.

Obediently, the elderly man cast the beads onto the lid. The men craned their necks forward to see the configuration of the beads, and all heads turned to the newcomer next to the captain. Rick could see over the men and saw five of the beads more or less lined up, with the purple one at the end, pointing to the man in the robe. The newcomer slumped in his place as the boat rolled suddenly to the port side, and the beads, the men, and Rick went flying.

"Tell us who you are, oh stranger," implored the captain, once he picked himself up, "and for what cause this evil is upon us."

The man remained silent for a few moments. "I am a despicable man," he said finally, his sullen voice leaden with despair. "My name is Jonah, son of Amittai. The lot has been well cast. I have offended the God of heaven and earth."

Jonah! Of course, Jonah! Rick thought to himself.

"What do you mean?" asked the captain earnestly. "What have you done?"

Agitation replaced some of the despair but none of the pain in Jonah's face. "The Lord commanded me to go to the Assyrians in Nineveh, to cry warning unto them. But I would not, for they are barbarians in heart and mind." At this, he cast a worried glance around the hold. Satisfied that there were no Assyrians in the group, he continued. "So I ran from the Lord and from his command. This is the cause of our calamity. The God of heaven and earth is wroth."

"Pray, tell me where do you come from?" asked the captain. "What is your country—from what people are you? Who is this God that you worship?"

"I am a Hebrew and fear Jehovah, the God of heaven, who made the sea and the dry land. It is he who is angry. His arm will not be stayed." At this, Jonah buried his face into his hands. "I have offended the Lord, and this is my recompense. I am condemned to die."

The boat suddenly plunged forward, sending Rick's stomach to his throat. The men, none of them restrained in harnesses, flew in a mass against the forward walls. The sea then bucked the ship over to its back, and pure bedlam broke out in the hold. The glass coverings that had been protecting candles that hung on the walls shattered, and all light was extinguished. At the same moment, the crates from the back portion of the hold burst from their restraints, crashed down onto the ceiling of the ship, which was for that moment the floor, and then began to hurdle violently in all directions as the ship tossed in the waves. It was two or three minutes before the ship miraculously righted itself once again, but the water in the hold was then almost knee deep.

The captain called out, "Oh, Hebrew, what must we do to calm the waters?"

"Take me up, and cast me forth into the sea," he answered. "Then shall the sea be calmed. For it is for my sake that this great tempest is upon you."

The captain looked at him warily. "We will not add to our troubles with your blood."

"Oarsmen, back to your posts!" he bellowed. "Bring us round to land!" The bare-chested men climbed a rope to the hatches in the ceiling and pushed them open, exposing for a moment the compartments below the deck and on each side of the hold where a few men could add the power of oars to the sail that normally propelled them.

But it was no use. The storm was too strong and the manpower too weak. And without a tiller on deck, it would have been difficult to guide the ship even under normal conditions. All the while, Jonah kept imploring them to cast him out to sea.

Finally, when the futility of the quest was plain, the captain and his men turned to Jonah. "We are left without choice, oh stranger. We will do as you say. But we beseech thee, O God of the Hebrews," the captain said, lifting his voice and his arms heavenward in the hold, his gray figure only faintly visible in the darkness, "we beseech thee, let us not perish for this man's life. And lay not upon us innocent blood, for thou, O Lord, hast done as it pleased thee."

At this, one of the men swiftly climbed the ladder to the

deck and released the lock on the hatch. He then scaled down the ladder and made way for Jonah.

Jonah hesitated, but a swift jolt of the boat and a prodding from the captain moved him up the ladder. Two of the men followed him, secured by ropes. Twenty seconds or so later the two of them dove back down the hatch, fastening the latch once again before dropping into the hold.

Jonah had been cast into the sea.[34]

10

WHO WE ARE

Exhausted, and amazed by what he had just witnessed, Rick was more confused than ever as to why he was there. "What is this about, Grandpa?" he asked again. "What is the point? What do you want me to learn?"

"Do you know the rest of Jonah's story, Ricky?"

"Sure, he gets swallowed by a big fish and after three days the fish spits him onto dry land, and then he goes to Nineveh and preaches after all, and the people repent and are preserved. I get it. I know the story. But I don't see what it has to do with *me*."

"That's why we're here, Ricky—so you *will* see."

The winds and waves had suddenly calmed, and the men ascended the ladder en masse. Rick and his grandfather followed them up. Once on deck, they surveyed the scene. The mast had been snapped off only a foot or two above the deck and the sail lost to the sea. Except for a few lonely pieces, the wicker fence had been almost entirely ripped away. But the twilight sky above was clear, and the water lay still as glass. The men dropped to their knees and offered prayers of thanksgiving.

Rick followed his grandfather to the bow and looked out across the now tranquil Mediterranean.

"Do you suppose that you've ever fled to Tarshish, Ricky?" his grandfather asked after a minute or two.

"Run from the Lord, you mean? No, I don't think so."

"No?" Grandpa asked, raising his eyebrows in Rick's direction. "Let's think about what it *means* to flee to Tarshish."

Great, here we go again, thought Rick. *More Socrates.*

"Yes, I suppose so, my boy," Grandpa said with a brief chuckle. "Let's think about what we have just witnessed. *Why* did Jonah flee to Tarshish?"

"For the reason I just said, to run from the Lord."

"That's what he was doing, fair enough, Ricky, but why? *Why* was he running from the Lord?"

"Because he didn't want to go to Nineveh, I suppose."

"Yes, but why?"

"I don't know, Grandpa! I guess he just didn't want to go. Maybe he didn't like them."

"You're right on both counts," Grandpa responded, ignoring Rick's agitation. "He didn't want to go, and he didn't like the Ninevites. And the reason he didn't is because of what they had done to his people, and what they were yet to do."

"What do you mean?"

"In Jonah's day, Nineveh was a major city within the Assyrian empire—soon to become its capital. The Assyrians were a brutal, war-mongering people, feared by all around them—including, I might add, the Phoenicians, like the sailors on this ship, who were required to pay tribute to Assyria in order to maintain their sovereignty.

"By this time in history, the Assyrian empire included almost all of present-day Iraq and Syria, and much of present-day Jordan and Turkey. For a time they even controlled Egypt. The Assyrians had been raiding the borders of the northern kingdom of Israel for years, collecting tribute from them as well. And Jonah knew from the words of fellow prophets that the Assyrians would soon destroy the northern kingdom and lead his people into captivity,[35] which happened in 721 B.C."

Grandpa paused for a moment, looking out to sea. "So how could Jonah work to save them?" he finally asked. "Why would the Lord even ask him to? That is what Jonah was stumbling over, Ricky. In his mind, Nineveh didn't *deserve* to be saved. And he, one of the aggrieved and mistreated, didn't deserve to be required to help them."

Rick remembered his grandfather's earlier comment about Rick feeling he deserved better from Carol. "So you think I'm like Jonah, then, is that it, Grandpa? You're saying that I'm upset because I think I deserve better than I'm getting, and in that respect I'm like Jonah."

His grandfather didn't say anything.

"Well, maybe I *am* then. But you know what? I can't blame Jonah, to tell you the truth, now that I know what he was facing. Who could blame him for not wanting to go to Nineveh? For not wanting to help the very people who soon would wipe out his own people without a second thought? So maybe I *am* like Jonah. That doesn't seem so bad to me, under the circumstances. It beats being Nineveh, I'd say."

"Actually, Ricky, that's who you are."

"Who?"

"Nineveh."

"I'm *Nineveh?*"

"Yes. And so, by the way, is Jonah. That's why we're here. *And* why Jonah is somewhere in *there,*" he said, nodding toward the sea.

11

WHAT WE DESERVE

Jow could Jonah be Nineveh?" Rick objected, thinking as
well of himself. "He's not a conqueror. He doesn't make
others' lives miserable. He's *nothing* like Nineveh. He's a
prophet, for heaven's sake."

"Actually, Ricky, he is *exactly* like Nineveh in the only way
that really matters."

"How so?"

"Remember, Jonah feels that Nineveh doesn't deserve to be
saved. That's why he's running. But guess who else doesn't
deserve to be saved?"

Grandpa Carson's question hung heavy in the salty air.

"You're saying that Jonah doesn't deserve to be saved
either," Rick finally responded. His voice trailed off at the
thought.

"Exactly. If Jonah demands that everybody gets only what they deserve, then he must also accept what *he* deserves. And, that, Ricky," he said, turning his eyes back to the sea, "is what he is now getting."

Grandpa fell silent and Rick became lost in his thoughts. *But what about Carol and how she treats me!* he bellowed within himself. *"Without charity ye are nothing"—that's what the scriptures say. And Carol is almost devoid of charity. She shouldn't be like that. I* deserve *better. Isn't that right?* Rick was confused. *Isn't that right?*

"Actually, you're both right and wrong," his grandfather interrupted, stepping again into Rick's thoughts. "It is true that we are commanded to love and honor others, and it is likely true that Carol fails always to do that—just as you and I fail. But what's false is this idea that you or I *deserve* that love and devotion—that we are somehow *entitled* to it. The truth is that there is only one thing we truly deserve, and that's to be sent to hell—you, Carol, me, Jonah, Nineveh, all of us. Love and salvation are gifts. How grateful we should be to receive them in any measure!" At that, Grandpa Carson again looked out across the sea.

"Hell is all we could ever hope for, Ricky, if it weren't for the redeeming power of the Savior's atonement. It is only his love, offered not because we deserve it but even though we do not, that saves us. We don't want what we deserve, believe me. Jonah is finding that out right now. Our only hope is to receive what we *don't* deserve—the mercy that brings the gift of eternal life. And Jonah is about to learn about that as well."

So am I wrong to think that Carol is wronging me? Is that what this means? Rick argued within himself. "There's something I don't understand, Grandpa," he objected. "I understand that without the Savior, we are all equally lost—you, me, Carol, Jonah, Nineveh. I understand that. But the fact is we're *not* without the Savior. And his atonement requires our righteousness—we are saved by grace 'after all we can do,'[36] right? So doesn't it matter in Jonah's case, for example, that he is more righteous than the Ninevites, notwithstanding this ill-fated run to Tarshish. Doesn't that mean *something?*"

"Yes, it does mean something, Ricky, but not what you think it does."

"You didn't use to speak in riddles, Grandpa," Rick chided.

Grandpa Carson's laugh cleared the tension Rick was beginning to feel. He turned to face Rick. "I'm sorry, my boy. I'm not trying to confuse you. Let me put it this way: Whether or not Nineveh is righteous is critical, of course—but only for Nineveh. It has nothing to do with Jonah. And if he thinks it does—if he thinks he is more deserving because he is somehow better than Nineveh, then he in that moment becomes more 'Ninevitish' than the people he is blaming."

"But what if the Ninevites *really are* bad?" Rick asked, thinking of his marriage. "What if Jonah *really is* better than they are? What if he *really is* more righteous? Why would it be a problem for Jonah just to acknowledge the truth?"

"Because he *wouldn't* be acknowledging the truth, Ricky, that's just the point. If he really is more righteous than they are, it will not occur to him to think that he is more righteous than they are because he will understand fully and deeply that he is entitled to nothing but hell. At least in one sense, 'righteousness' is simply a humble understanding of how unrighteous one is, coupled with a deep commitment to be better. The truth leaves no room for feelings of superiority. Such feelings are nothing but lying vanities."

These words settled on Rick with such force that he gave up his project of reloading arguments. He hadn't realized until that moment that his main object so far with his grandfather had been to be "right," and that he had made most of their time together into a kind of verbal jousting match. Something about this last comment, or perhaps it was the way his grandfather had said it—Rick wasn't sure—changed everything. He felt his toes relax, and he settled into his feet. The tension evaporated from his face and neck, and he turned to look out to sea with his grandfather.

"You see, Ricky, relative righteousness means nothing. Whether Jonah was better or worse than Nineveh isn't the question at all, is it? And whether you are better or worse than Carol isn't the question either. Some laborers work longer, the Savior told us in one of his parables, and others shorter.[37] Each person's payment at the end of the day has nothing whatsoever to do with the work of others. We are each working out our own salvation with fear and trembling before the Lord. And that gift will come to us only if we know in our hearts that we deserve it no more than anyone else. What I meant earlier by 'fleeing to Tarshish' was just this: persisting in the idea that we are better, more righteous, and deserve more than others. The truth is, we are all, each of us, equally damned without the mercy of the Lord. Eternal life is a gift. I have no cause to feel entitled. I have cause only to feel grateful."

"Yeah, I guess that's right," Rick agreed, heaving a heavy sigh. "But it's just so difficult, Grandpa. I'm really struggling." For the first time since he found himself on the ship, Rick let down his defenses and opened his heart.

"Carol and I aren't good together, Grandpa," he lamented. "I don't respond well to her at all anymore. Every tiny injustice feels like it weighs a thousand pounds." Rick kept looking out to sea, his eyes glazing over as his mind wallowed in recent events. "A week ago, for example, I started cooking dinner after work, which I've had to do more and more over the last couple of years as Carol has basically thrown in the towel on preparing meals. Anyway, I thought I'd make some scrambled eggs and started mixing them in a bowl. Carol sat at the kitchen table while I did this, never offering help. And then, just before I dumped the eggs in the pan she told me to be sure to put butter in the pan so the eggs wouldn't stick so much. I protested a bit, I suppose, and she said, 'Look, it makes the pans really difficult to clean if you don't use butter. If you want to clean the mess yourself, then go ahead and do whatever you want.' That's what she said.

"And you know what?" Rick asked, more to himself than to his grandfather. "I just went off on her. I'd had enough. 'Why is there always a problem with what I do!' I demanded. 'Why can't you be grateful that I'm cooking dinner to begin with! Why can't you just be grateful!' And of course, I wasn't grateful when I said it. I felt entitled to a well-cooked meal, and if I couldn't have that, then I was entitled to cook in any way I pleased." Rick's eyes started to water at the futility of the memory. "She can't even ask me to use butter anymore," he sighed, his eyes filling with tears. "We can't even talk about eggs." Rick shook his head pathetically.

"Jonah knows well the despair that grips you, Ricky. But the Lord is about to teach him the way to escape from despair. Part one of that lesson now has Jonah in his belly.

"Part two awaits him in Nineveh."

12

A MERCIFUL QUESTION

R ick found himself with his grandfather on a hillside overlooking a vast valley plain. Behind him rose foothills that
developed into a substantial mountain range a few miles in the
distance. Below him spread a great city that rose from the banks
of a large river some fifteen miles away and spread from there
in all directions. The congested center area of the city, in and
of itself at least ten miles square and surrounded by a large
wall, was filled with whitish homes and buildings that appeared
to be stacked nearly on top of each other, they were so close.
Narrow, winding roads cut paths through the whitewashed
structures. A number of much larger buildings, governmental
in nature, Rick surmised, broke the boxy monotony of the
lesser structures.

In the center and toward the river rose a building many

times larger than any other. Rick couldn't tell because of the distance, but the base of this immense building looked to be a squat pyramid that itself rose above the other buildings, forming a massive foundation for the magnificent temple-like structure that rested upon it.

The city gradually decreased in density in all directions but continued as far as Rick could see on his side of the river. The outer areas eventually melded into farms, with homes and other buildings clustered here and there among harvested fields. The fields nearer Rick lay dry and burnt under the scorching sun, but in the distance, nearer the river, the ground still danced with color.

"So this is Nineveh," Rick said matter-of-factly.

"Yes, the great city," his grandfather responded. "The river beyond is the Tigris. We're about 230 miles north of present-day Baghdad, 550 miles northeast of Jerusalem.[38]

"Look," his grandfather said, pointing to their right.

Rick stepped forward to see beyond a boulder that was blocking his view. About twenty yards away stood a makeshift lean-to. A man was seeking shelter within it, mostly unsuccessfully, as there was little vegetation around them with which to fill in the cracks between sticks. A vine that grew up the sides and stretched over the top of the booth was withered and dying. "Jonah?" Rick asked.

"Yes. He climbed to this spot after preaching to the Ninevites as he had been commanded to do. 'Forty days,' he told them, 'and you will be destroyed unless you repent.'[39] He repeated his warning over the days and weeks that followed, the announced date of calamity marching ever nearer. Jonah *liked* delivering that message, Ricky, for he was eager for the Ninevites' destruction. The worse they and their prospects were, the happier it made him feel. He enjoyed his role as 'prophet.' But to his surprise and chagrin, the Ninevites repented and the Lord withdrew his sentence.

"Yesterday was the fortieth day from Jonah's initial warning. He has spent the last twenty-four hours demanding that the Lord follow through on his initial word and destroy the Ninevites. Jonah remains on this hillside to witness that hoped-for destruction."

"But the Lord *doesn't* destroy them."

"No, Ricky, he doesn't. And Jonah's story is about to end right here on this hill, with an angry Jonah baking under those sticks, and the Lord waiting for an answer to a question."

"What question?"

Grandpa Carson smiled. "A question that was intended as much for you and for me as for Jonah."

"What do you mean?"

"The book of Jonah ends with a question, a question the Lord asks of Jonah. But the scriptural record stops before Jonah answers. Jonah's answer is omitted because his answer is important only to Jonah. The question remains for us *unanswered*, as the Lord poses it to each reader anew. The Lord now asks that question of you, Ricky. And your answer—today, and in every moment hereafter—will determine whether you will remain gripped by despair or find your way to joy."

"What's the question?" Rick asked with more urgency.

"'Should not I spare Nineveh?'"[40]

That's it? Rick wondered. "I'm not seeing the profundity, Grandpa. What am I missing?"

"You are missing Carol, my boy. And four children whose pains you do not know."

These words took Rick's breath away more fully than the scorching east wind that suddenly engulfed him.

"I want to show you something," Grandpa Carson said, walking over to pick up a small stick that lay a few feet from them. Having retrieved it, he returned to where Rick was standing and squatted to the earth.

"There is something about the Jonah story that you should know," he said, digging the stick deep enough through the sand to preserve the words despite the wind. After he had finished he said, "Look at this."

He had written the following:

1. The Lord commands Jonah to preach against the wicked Ninevites.

2. Jonah sins, not wanting Nineveh to be saved.

3. Jonah repents and the Lord saves Jonah.

3. Nineveh repents and the Lord saves Nineveh.

2. Jonah sins, not wanting Nineveh to be saved.

1. The Lord asks Jonah a question: Should not I spare Nineveh?

"This, Ricky, is the story of Jonah. Do you notice anything about it?"

"Yes. The elements of the story repeat themselves in reverse order. It's a chiasm—an ordering structure prevalent in Hebrew writing."

"Very good, Ricky," said his grandfather, obviously impressed. "I didn't know about chiasms until I came *here*," he said—referring, Rick surmised, to the hereafter, and not specifically to the hill above Nineveh.

"Then you know, Ricky," he continued, "that chiastic writings differ from linear writings in this respect: Chiastic passages point inward, to the center. The end of a chiastic story is not so much the end as it is an invitation to consider the center anew. With that in mind, let's think about the chiasm's closing element, the Lord's question, 'Should not I spare Nineveh?' What do you notice in the center?"

"Well, in both of the center elements the Lord delivered salvation. First he saved Jonah, and then he saved Nineveh."

"Exactly. The Lord saved Jonah and Nineveh alike, and on the same terms—repentance. So if Jonah's answer to the Lord's question is, 'No, the Ninevites, who you have saved, shouldn't be saved,' who, then, by implication, must also not be saved?"

"Jonah," Rick answered, almost in a whisper. His mind raced trying to put the pieces together. "You're saying that if Jonah can't be happy at the thought of Nineveh's salvation, then he makes *himself* unworthy of salvation."

"Yes. Or perhaps I would put it this way: Jonah is *already* unworthy of salvation, as is Nineveh. *No one* merits it. Salvation is an act of mercy. The Lord poses his question in terms of mercy for Nineveh, but mercy for Nineveh is no longer in question. The mercy that remains in question is mercy for Jonah. The implication of the Lord's question is this: Mercy can be extended only to those who are willing to extend it themselves.

"The Lord's question to Jonah is the same one he posed in the parable of the unmerciful servant, whose debt the lord—his master—had forgiven: 'Shouldest not thou also have had compassion on thy fellowservant, even as I had pity on thee?' the lord asked. 'And his lord was wroth,' the Savior taught, 'and delivered him to the tormentors. . . . So likewise,' the Savior continued, 'shall my heavenly Father do also unto you, if ye from your hearts forgive not every one his brother their trespasses.'"[41]

Rick's shoulders slumped a little as he considered his marriage in light of what his grandfather was saying.

"It's no accident, Ricky, that the very center statement of the book of Jonah, which appears in the middle of the center elements of the chiasm, with twenty-four verses preceding it and twenty-three verses following, reads: 'They that observe lying vanities forsake their own mercy.'[42] Jonah sits in that booth observing lying vanities: He has forgotten his own prior sin; he has forgotten the mercy extended to him by the mariners, who tried to spare him even when they knew he was the cause of their troubles; he has forgotten the ultimate mercy of the Lord, who delivered *him* even though he didn't deserve it; and he is therefore blind to his own 'Nineveh-ness'—to how he, himself, is Nineveh. Failing to see mercifully, his heart, mind, and eyes are lying to him. All he can see is that he is 'right,' 'entitled,' 'deserving.' Observing 'lying vanities,' he is in danger of 'forsaking his own mercy.' And feeling no personal mercy, he is locked in despair.

"Which leads me to this question, Ricky: Is there any way that you are forgetting your own sins? Any way that you are failing to remember mercies that Carol has showed you? Any way that you are forgetting the Lord? Any way that you have become blind to your own 'Nineveh-ness'? Any way that you persist in feeling entitled?

"Your escape from despair lies in your answer to these questions."

13

MERCY IN THE BALANCE

B ut how *can* it, Grandpa? Those questions only make me feel worse."

"That is exactly why they hold the key to joy."

"That doesn't make sense."

"In a different day and age it would have, Ricky, but not in your day, when everyone is trying to find happiness without giving up their sins. But you and I know better: 'Wickedness never was happiness.'[43] King Benjamin's people became filled with joy only after they fell to the earth in fear for their sins, viewing themselves as 'less than the dust of the earth.'[44] The despair that gripped Alma the younger was replaced by joy only after he was 'harrowed up by the memory of his many sins.'[45] The father of King Lamoni had it right when he prayed, 'I will give away all my sins to know thee,'[46] which required him to recognize what was sinful within him.

"And so I ask again: Are there any ways that you are forgetting your *own* sins? Any ways you are failing to remember mercies that Carol has showed you? Any ways that you are forgetting the Lord? Any ways that you have become blind to your own 'Nineveh-ness'? Any ways that you persist in feeling entitled? Contrary to modern belief, there are no happier questions than these."

Rick's mind was by now far away in a memory. He was sitting in the driver's seat of his car, Carol next to him. They had been out on a date that night—more from a feeling of obligation than from a desire to be together. Their conversations had been forced and awkward. They were now headed home, far earlier than on any date before they were married, in order to save on the baby-sitter bill. The penny-pinching reason for their early return, so common in their marriage, gnawed at Rick, but on this night he was anxious to get home himself, where rooms and walls would muffle the painful echo of their silence.

"There's something I need to say to you," Carol had said as they neared their home. To which Rick thought, *Great, here we go again.*

"I'm not very strong right now," Carol began. *"It isn't fair to you, I suppose, but you are going to have to supply the love and understanding and support in this relationship. I'm afraid that I can't do it right now."*

Rick pulled the car to a stop on the shoulder of the road. *"That isn't fair, Carol,"* he retorted, flashing her an angry look.

"You can't demand that of me. You can't just say that you're not strong enough to supply love right now. You can't do that! It's not right. I'm not feeling very strong either, to tell you the truth. Who's going to give me the support that I need! Hmm?"

"I know it isn't fair, Rick, and I'm really sorry about it." Rick recalled the self-pitying look on her face, and he felt repulsed anew.

"'Sorry'! This is what you mean by sorry? That's no apology, Carol. And besides, you can't get what you're looking for the way you're trying to get it, anyway. You don't discover love by demanding love from others. You discover it by learning to love others yourself. Unless you find a way to love, my love, or anyone else's, won't help you. You discover love by learning to love others. There is no other way."

"Truer words have never been spoken, Ricky," his grandfather interrupted, ripping Rick back from his memory. "Too bad you didn't believe what you were saying."

"Huh? What do you mean?"

"You told Carol that 'you don't discover love by demanding love from others, you discover it by learning to love others.' And how right you were. But you didn't believe it even when you said it."

"Sure I did. I *still* believe it."

"Do you?"

"Yes. Absolutely."

"Then tell me, if you believed that your love of others does not depend on their love of you, why did you have a problem with Carol's request? Why did you get upset when she said that she was feeling weak and that you were going to have to be the primary source of love and support for awhile?"

"Well, because it isn't right, that's why."

"*What* isn't right?"

"That one person—me—has to supply all the love. It isn't fair! I'm tired of it. Why can't she hold up her end?"

"Do you need her to?"

"Yes."

"Why?"

"*Why?*" Rick repeated, incredulously. "*Why?*"

"Yes, why?"

"Well, *because.* Because we're married and we're supposed to be 'one'—one flesh and one heart. Are you saying that she doesn't have to love me? That it's just tough luck and deal with it? If so, I disagree completely. That isn't what marriage should be like!"

"You're quite right, Ricky, that isn't what marriage should be like. But it is also clear from what you've just said that you don't believe what you told Carol. Your own love *is* contingent on hers—you say you are willing to be 'one,' but only if *she* is. And if *your* love is contingent on *hers,* then why shouldn't *hers* be contingent on *yours?*"

"But what are you saying, then, Grandpa? That I should just smile and be happy? I'm sorry; I'm not going to do that. I won't be taken advantage of, by Carol or anyone else. I saw what that was like by watching you and Grandma. I won't have it that way."

Grandpa Carson paused for a moment and looked up at the sky. A bead of sweat trickled down his brow, the first sign of stress that Rick had witnessed during their encounters. He shook his head slowly. "I'm not sure I can help you, Ricky," he said. "I'm not sure I can help."

Rick had fallen back into defensiveness, but this comment shook him free. "What do you mean, Grandpa?"

"Just what I said, my boy. I'm not sure I can help you. Perhaps another time," he said, standing tall and turning toward Rick, "when you're ready." He tried to give Rick a smile.

"No. Don't go. I'm not ready for you to go. I want to understand this. Please stay. I'm sorry about what I just said. I didn't mean it, not really."

Grandpa Carson looked deeply into Rick's eyes. As Rick returned the look, he saw for the first time a profound sadness in those eyes, as if a lifetime's worth of tears had pooled up in a place deep within.

"What's wrong, Grandpa?"

"I love you so much, Ricky. In the same measure that I love your Carol. It's almost more than I can bear to see you both suffer. And at each other's hands—" He broke off what he was saying and looked out over the expanse of Nineveh. "And your children too—Alan, Eric, Anika, and Lauren—don't be fooled by their smiles and silence, Ricky; they know what's going on, Alan and Eric in particular."

Rick felt like he'd been kicked in the stomach.

"They've heard many of your arguments while pretending to sleep, perhaps as you heard things not intended for your ears when you stayed with me and Grandma." He cast Rick a knowing look.

"They have spent many tearful nights because of what they have heard," he continued. "They're confused, Ricky, and worried. You have no idea the pain they feel. They hide it well because they love you so much.

"You know how eager they are to see you every night?" he asked.

Rick nodded absentmindedly.

"You think they are just happy to see you. And they *are*, to be sure, but there is more to it than that. They are trying to hold the family together, and they do that in part by holding you themselves. There is desperation as well as love in their arms and fingers."

The memories of those eager hugs flooded Rick's mind, and he nearly doubled over in pain as he felt the long embraces anew. He could feel the fear in those clutches, just as his grandfather said. *Why didn't I notice it before?*

"Every prayer Alan and Eric have offered up over the last year has centered around you, Carol, and the family," his grandfather continued. "In fact, it is because of them, and their prayers, that I am here."

Rick couldn't find a word to say. He thought of Alan and Eric, Anika and Lauren. *They couldn't have really been hurt, could they?* he hoped lamely out of his own desperation. *Please, Lord, don't let them be hurt.*

"Perhaps you can learn something from how they are dealing with that hurt," came his grandfather's voice. "The desperate love they are showing both you and Carol, as a way of holding the family together, can help you with your struggle if you will let it."

"How?"

"Consider, Ricky, how your children are answering the Lord's question, 'Should not I spare Nineveh?' Like the Phoenician mariners, they have done nothing wrong yet suffer for the wrongs of others. And despite the fact that they have done nothing wrong—despite the fact that they have done nothing to deserve the pain they are feeling—they love you with all their hearts. They desperately pray for your happiness. They beg for the Lord's mercy on your behalf. Their love is not contingent on yours or Carol's. It does not fail in the face of difficulty.

"When you discover why that is," he continued, "your love will no longer be contingent either, and you will experience a love that you have only fleetingly known, a love that endureth forever and faileth not, despite hardships and difficulties. When you discover that love, you will discover a Carol that you haven't known either. Your answer to the Lord's question will then be the right one, and despair will give way to hope and joy."

14

WAITING FOR AN ANSWER

Grandpa Carson waited for a moment for some kind of a response, but Rick stood silently in thought.

"Let me put it this way, Ricky: Your children are suffering terribly in your home, as you are. Yet they are able to love those at whose hands they suffer, while you are struggling to do so. Why the difference, do you suppose? What difference between you and your children would explain the difference in your abilities to love?"

"Well, they're mere innocents, Grandpa," Rick said quickly. "They don't know enough to know better."

"Is your way the better way, Ricky?" his grandfather said in a large voice that seemed to overpower the wind. "Are you the one who knows the truth here? If your children were more knowledgeable, would they then know better than to love those who mistreat them? Is *that* your answer? Is *that* the enlightenment your children need?"

Grandpa Carson's eyes flashed, and Rick cowered under their scrutiny and the force of his grandfather's voice and conviction.

"Perhaps it is *you* who no longer knows enough, Ricky. Perhaps it is *you* who needs the education. And who better to teach you than those who suffer because of you."

Rick felt tears begin to well up inside of him, both because his grandfather was so clearly disappointed in him and because he had so disappointed his children. He choked back the tears, half successfully, as his lids held the water from streaming down his cheeks.

"You said your children were mere innocents," said Grandpa Carson, his voice now back to its normal volume and cadence. "With that statement you come so close to understanding something profound yet end up so far from it."

He paused for a moment. "I want to ask you a question, Ricky. Who in the scriptures comes to mind as someone who was able to love others even though he was despised and abused by them?"

"The Savior, of course."

"Have you ever wondered how he was able to do this?"

"Well, yes, but I don't think we can begin to fathom the reasons. He is the Son of God, after all."

"So it was his pedigree, then? It was because of his genes

that he was able to love those who caused him to suffer—is that it?"

"Well, no, not exactly."

"No, it wouldn't seem so, would it, as he commands us—no matter who our fathers and mothers may be—to love, just as he was able to, those who despitefully use us and persecute us. And if he commands us to love in just that way, then it's pretty important that we understand why he was able to do so himself, wouldn't you say?"

"Yes," Rick answered soberly.

"Well, let's think about it, then. When you think about the Savior and what he did for us, what strikes you as particularly remarkable about him?"

"Everything," Rick said, quite honestly.

"Let's get specific."

"Okay—well, he suffered for all of our sins, as we talked about with Abigail and David."

"Yes, good. What else?"

"He loves all mankind, saint and sinner alike."

"Yes, that's right. Excellent. And what else?"

"Maybe the most amazing thing of all is that he never did anything wrong."

"Exactly, Ricky, he never sinned toward anyone—including those who caused him to suffer. He never sinned at all."

Grandpa Carson dipped his head down to intercept Rick's

gaze. "Now," he said, having secured his attention, "do you notice anything similar about your children?"

Rick pondered for a moment. "Yes. They also love those who are causing them to suffer," he lamented, his ache returning.

"Yes, they do. Anything else?"

"Like Christ, they're not doing wrong toward me or Carol, either. Is that what you want me to say?"

"Ricky, what you *say* is only marginally important to me. What I care most about is how you *feel* about what you say. But let's deal first with your words. Remember how you said that your children were 'mere innocents'?"

Rick nodded.

"This is what I meant by you being close to a crucial under-standing and yet so far away: The important difference between you and your children is not that your children are *innocents* but that they are *innocent*—that is, they are not doing wrong toward those who are creating difficulties for them."

"What difference would *that* make?"

"What difference indeed," his grandfather answered ponderously.

Rick hesitated. "I don't understand, Grandpa. Why would that be the critical difference? And if it is, how could I ever hope for things to be better than they are? I'm not perfect, you know, and I'm not likely to be."

"Your children aren't perfect, either, Ricky. But such love is nevertheless found in them."

"Then that cuts against what you just said: they're imperfect, so they're not innocent either. We're not different in that respect at all."

"Ah, now we're to the point," his grandfather said, almost to himself. "Think of Jonah over there," he said, gesturing beyond the rock.

Rick turned to look at the limp figure under the sticks. There he sat, still slumped under the heat of the sun.

"He is a bitter man at the moment. He thinks he is in the 'right' here. In fact, he is so convinced of it, he's willing to face off against the Lord. His is the cause of justice. Meanwhile, the Lord's question hangs in the air, 'Should not I spare Nineveh?'[47]

"What do you suppose would happen, Ricky, if Jonah were to give up his belligerence and answered, both in word and feeling, 'Yes!'? Do you suppose he would sit the same way under those sticks? Do you suppose his countenance would remain sour? Do you suppose he would continue to curse at the sun? Do you suppose he would feel the way he currently does about Nineveh?"

"No, probably not," Rick answered.

"His world would change, wouldn't it—not because he would be perfect but because he would recognize in that moment that he has no claim to perfection in others, that his and others' hopes rest entirely on mercy, that he is entitled to nothing and grateful for everything. In that moment, he wouldn't become perfect, but he *would* become innocent—

innocent because he would have allowed the Lord's offered mercy to well up inside of and change him into a new man, free from the clutches of sin."

Grandpa turned back to Rick. "Notice something, Ricky. Jonah sits on this hill believing that the world will improve for the better only if there is some drastic change in Nineveh. David felt the same way about Nabal. That is why he started marching to Carmel—to inflict that drastic change. But David discovered through Abigail that the change that meant everything was not a change in Nabal but a change in himself—a change that is invited by the Lord's question. The Lord is now offering Jonah the same discovery. The drastic changes we just imagined in Jonah don't depend on Nineveh at all. Jonah is unhappy for one reason and one reason alone, and it is not the reason he thinks: Like David, he is unhappy not because of another's sins but because of his own.

"This understanding is available merely from pondering the Savior's atonement, for no amount of mistreatment and suffering was able to take away the love of One who was without sin. By contrast, we who still struggle with sinfulness, struggle as well to cover our sins.[48] And one way we do this, the Savior taught, is by finding sinfulness in others. The beams in our eyes get us looking for the motes in others'.[49] Our own failure to love another causes us to see the other as being unworthy of love. So we end up sitting beneath our own canopies of sticks—irritated, angry, hurt—blaming our lack of love on the Ninevites *we are failing to love.* The Savior, by contrast, with no sins of his own to clutch, cover, and excuse, remained free to see all of mankind—each of us Ninevite in our sinfulness and in the pain we caused him—mercifully and gratefully.

"Your children answer 'Yes' to the Lord's question, Ricky. They grant mercy to the Ninevites in their home, by throwing their arms around Nineveh every night. The secret of their love is not their naiveté—the fact that they are, as you said, mere *innocents*—but is rather their *innocence* from sin. Innocent as they are from sinfulness toward you, there are no sins they need to cover and excuse, and therefore no sins of yours can keep them from loving you.

"The question for you is what sins toward Carol keep you from loving her? How are you demanding justice and therefore denying mercy? In what ways are you sitting belligerently under the sticks of your own grudges? How are you the author of your own despair? If you allow yourself to discover answers to those questions, you, with your children, will answer 'Yes!' to the Lord's question, and rediscover a Carol who is much less like Nineveh than you think she is—a Carol whom your children love every bit as much as they love you."

His grandfather wiped his brow and looked eastward toward the mountains. "It's time for me to go, Ricky. I leave you now with Jonah, and with his question. The city before you, as wicked as Jonah thinks it is, is saved. Will *you* be? Will *he*? That will depend entirely upon how you and he see the other Ninevites in your lives."

"I have faith in you, Son," he added after a brief pause. "You know the right, and you'll find the way. I know you will."

"Thanks, Grandpa. I hope you're right. I'm not so sure."

His grandfather took Rick in his arms in a warm embrace, the way he used to when Rick was about to go back home after a summer on the farm. "Good-bye, Son."

"Good-bye, Grandpa. Will I see you again?"

"Perhaps."

"I hope so." Rick bit his lip to keep the tears at bay.

Grandpa Carson smiled, nodded his head, and said, "As much as I'd like that, my greatest hope is that you will see Carol again—as you used to, as the Lord sees her, as she *is*."

With that, his grandfather set off for the mountains. He paused on the top of the next hill to the east and called, "Remember the Lord's question, Ricky. And remember that no one is more Ninevite than you are."

And then he was gone. Rick was alone with Jonah on the hillside, the sun beating mercilessly upon their heads.

PART III

THE CHAINS
OF SIN

15

A NEW DAY

Rick squinted as sunlight poured in through the window. The storm had passed, finally. Carol was already out of bed and probably on her morning walk. He looked past where she normally would have been to the clock on her nightstand. It was 7:50 A.M. He panicked for a moment until he remembered it was Saturday. Shedding the comforter, he rested under the sheet and gazed at the ceiling.

Yesterday felt like a long time ago. So much had happened overnight that Rick was struggling to fit it all together. And did he ever have a lot to fit together! He remembered his friend's advice about waking impressions and hopped out of bed to find some paper. Having found some in his nightstand, he reclined on the bed and started to sift through what he had seen.

The stories of Abigail and Jonah swam in his mind. He could sense that their messages were connected, but he struggled to piece them together. He looked for the logic.

He thought about mercy and justice, about feeling grateful or entitled. He relived the scene on the road to Carmel and remembered Jonah on the boat and under the canopy of sticks. *Abigail was a type of Christ,* he recalled. He remembered his grandfather saying that her story illuminates the Lord's atonement from a different angle than we normally think about. *But what angle was that?* He strained to remember. *Oh yes, that the Lord has paid in full for others' sins, that was the point—that it may be helpful to think more often about how he has paid for others' sins rather than just dwelling on how he has paid for our own.*

What do we see in the atonement when we look at it from that angle? Then he remembered how Abigail, in her role as peace-maker, claimed Nabal's sins and asked David to forgive <u>her</u>. *How could he ever withhold forgiveness from her?* And that was just the point, for he hadn't.

Then there was the point about how Abigail supplied David with everything he needed, thereby atoning for another's sins and making David whole. *Yes, that's right,* he assured himself. *That makes sense. But what about Jonah? What does his story have to do with Abigail's?*

Rick puzzled about that. And then he realized that, of course, the Jonah and Abigail stories were each about extending mercy and therefore intersected on that point. *But how do they*

illuminate different aspects of mercy? he wondered. Rick continued this way for a few minutes and then tried to record his
thinking in some logical way—in a form he could understand
and remember. He was genuinely excited, some forty-five minutes later, when he looked at what he had finally written:

THE LORD'S ATONEMENT AND MERCY

1. We are each of us sinners, entitled to nothing but
hell and therefore utterly and equally dependent upon
the mercies of the Lord. (Jonah)

2. I can receive of the Lord's mercy—and the happiness, healing, and peace that attend it—only to the
extent I extend the same to others. (Jonah)

3. The Lord mercifully removes any justification for
failing to extend mercy to others. (Abigail)

   a. For the Lord has taken the sins of others
   upon his own head and personally atoned for
   them. (Abigail)

   b. What possible justification could there
   be for demanding more for others' sins than the
   Lord has given? (Abigail)

4. I can recover mercy by remembering (a) Abigail's
offering, (b) the Lord's question to Jonah, and (c) my
own sins, the memory of which brings me to the Lord
and invites me to rediscover his mercy and peace.

5. If I repent of failing to extend mercy, the Lord

will supply me with everything I need and more—he will grant me his love, his companionship, his understanding, his support. He will make my burdens light. (Abigail)

Rick read and reread what he had written. As he did so, he felt a hope within him that he hadn't felt in months, if not years. Happiness was still a possibility, and it had more to do with him than he had imagined.

He could hear the TV downstairs. *The kids must be up.* He sprang out of bed, pulled on some clothes, and folded the paper into his pocket. It was time to rejoin his family.

16

THE STORM RENEWED

The family room was a disaster. Anika and Lauren were watching cartoons. They had made a bed in the middle of the floor with the pillows from both couches. The reading chair, which had been turned upside down, was the center support for a large tent that utilized at least five blankets and covered the far half of the room. Puzzle pieces—Anika's favorite pastime—were strewn all around the floor and into the kitchen.

"Hi, girls. Kind of messy, huh?"

They stayed glued to the TV and said nothing.

"Anika, good morning."

"Hi, Dad."

She still didn't turn from the TV.

"Did you sleep well?"

"Yeah."

Still 100 percent program.

"Where are the boys?"

No response.

"Anika! The boys—where are they?"

"Downstairs," she answered, her eyes glazed over.

Anika had yet to even look at him, but Lauren turned and flashed him her big, mischievous grin. "Hi, Daddy."

Rick couldn't help but smile. "Hi, sweetheart. Sleep well?"

"Uh huh." She raised her eyebrows, turned her eyes sideways and up in their sockets (all without moving her head), and looked up toward the ceiling.

"Do you remember coming in to me last night?"

"Yep." Her little tongue almost poked through her cheek.

Rick just laughed. No one could say so much while saying so little. "I'm going to go find the boys, okay, honey?"

"Okay, Daddy," she said brightly, before whirling her head back to the TV. "I'm going to watch my show." Rick descended the basement stairs, chuckling to himself.

Alan and Eric were seated directly in front of the basement TV playing video games.

"Hey, guys."

"Hi, Dad," they said, almost in unison. Like Anika, they kept their eyes glued to the screen.

"I've got you now!" Alan blurted to Eric.

"Do you know where Mom is?" Rick interrupted.

"She's over at the Murrays'."

"What's she doing over there?"

"Oh! I can't believe that! That's not fair!" Alan yelled, elbowing Eric, who was smiling in satisfaction.

"Alan, what's she doing over there?" Rick repeated.

"They needed their children watched or something for awhile," he answered as if on autopilot. "I think Mr. and Mrs. Murray had to go to the airport or something.

"Take *that!*" he added to Eric, punctuating his words with a jerk of his controls.

The Murrays were always needing something, Rick thought to himself. And Carol could never say "No," so she did more than her share for them—more than she *should* do for them. And very often more than she seemed willing to do for *him,* he thought.

"So who's winning?" Rick asked.

"I am!" each shouted in unison.

"I get the winner."

An hour or so later Rick could hear Carol's footsteps on the kitchen floor upstairs. "We'd better finish up here, guys. Mom's home."

As Rick climbed the stairs he felt a little apprehensive, although he wasn't sure why. He had thought he wanted to see her, but he could already feel himself wanting to avoid her eyes. He had to force a smile a little when he entered the kitchen.

"Hi, Carol," he said, unable to call her "honey" or "hun," as were their common expressions for each other.

"Hi."

"So you were at the Murrays'?"

"Yes. They called last night and needed help."

Rick just nodded.

"I couldn't do anything about it, Rick. They needed help."

"I didn't say they didn't."

"No, but you were thinking it."

"No, I wasn't," Rick lied. "But they always seem to call *you*, don't they?"

"So? I think we should be more thoughtful of others than we are."

They were only twenty seconds into their day together and Rick, despite all the epiphanies of the night before, could feel many of his standard feelings bubbling up inside of him. "So I don't meet your standard of thoughtfulness either."

"I didn't say that."

"On the contrary, you couldn't have been more clear."

Carol shook her head in disgust.

Meanwhile, Alan and Eric had hesitated on the top stair as they heard their parents. They now entered the room softly and walked over to join their sisters in the family room.

"What's your problem, Rick?" she blurted, once the boys had seated themselves in the other room.

"Oh, you're a piece of work, Carol. It's always *my* problem, isn't it? I'm never good enough, am I?"

"I didn't say that. Quit saying that."

"If you don't like hearing it, how do you think *I* feel?"

"I have no idea how you feel," she snapped. "You never tell me. If I didn't bring things up, I swear we'd never talk."

"If this is what you mean by talking, we're probably better off not doing it, don't you think?"

At that, Carol stormed up the stairs.

Rick stood in the kitchen, his hands quivering with rage, his heart again mired in despair.

17

A BEAM OF LIGHT

Other than the TV in the next room, the house now stood in heavy silence—not accidental silence, but purposeful, scared, motivated silence.

Carol was somewhere upstairs—perhaps buried behind the clothes in their closet as Rick had sometimes found her. Wherever she was, she was surely feeling deeply sorry for herself. *Always sorry for _herself_,* Rick raged. *Never sorry for others, just for herself.* He clenched his teeth in anger, completely blind to the irony of his own self-pity.

"Daddy?"

It was Lauren, poking her head around the kitchen counter. Rick hadn't heard her approaching.

"Daddy," she said timidly, "will the hurties get better?"

"'Hurties'? What do you mean, honey?"

"Are Mommy's hurties going to get better?"

"'Mommy's hurties'?" Rick repeated lamely.

"Yes, on her heart. She showed me. Will she be all right, Daddy?"

Lauren's halting words and worried eyes melted Rick. He felt the anger drain from him, and he sat down on the floor and took her into his arms.

"Sure, sweetie," he said, stroking her tangled hair, "Mommy's hurties will be fine." His words were sure, but his heart wasn't. He loved his children so much, but he was feeling lost once more.

Rick held Lauren for a good minute, stroking her hair all the while. "Mom's pretty lucky to have a girl like you, isn't she?" he said, finally.

Lauren nodded in a much more subdued way than was natural for her.

"Go play with Anika and your brothers now. Everything will be fine."

Lauren obediently did as she was told, and Rick took his folded notes out of his pocket.

This didn't help much, he thought to himself in disgust, as he reread the words he had written that morning.

1. We are each of us sinners, entitled to nothing but hell and therefore utterly and equally dependent upon the mercies of the Lord. (Jonah)

Okay, I understand that, he thought.

2. I can receive of the Lord's mercy—and the happiness, healing, and peace that attend it—only to the
extent I extend the same to others. (Jonah)

But it isn't fair! What about mercy from Carol! But then he
read the next point:

3. The Lord mercifully removes any justification for
failing to extend mercy to others. (Abigail)
    a. For the Lord has taken the sins of others
upon his own head and personally atoned for
them. (Abigail)
    b. What possible justification could there
be for demanding more for others' sins than the
Lord has given? (Abigail)

Rick closed his eyes and leaned his head back against the
cupboard. *"Forgive me this trespass." That's what the Lord is saying here. "Forgive me this trespass."* He remembered David's
rigid form as he stood over Abigail. He recalled seeing the tension leave David's hands and face, and the calm serenity that
replaced it. David had been pierced by Abigail and her offering. He was able to let it all go. *Why can't I?* he cried within.
And, referring to Carol, *why can't she?*

    But the Jonah story says that it isn't about others at all, Rick
battled within. *Just like it wasn't about Nabal, either. My peace is*

not determined by others—whether they be righteous or not—but by myself. Or rather, my peace is determined by whether I come to Christ myself. For when I come to him, he blesses me with his mercy, and basking in that mercy I find peace. Whether others come to Christ—Nineveh and Nabal, for example—will determine their peace but not mine.

But she makes it harder! He shot back at himself. *It would be easier to come to Christ if she herself were better.*

Would it? came a voice from within.

Yes, absolutely.

Is that what the Book of Mormon teaches—that people come to the Lord most when things are easiest?

Rick's shoulders slumped. He had to concede—that's not what the Book of Mormon teaches. The Nephites came most readily to Christ when things were hardest and their burdens were greatest.

But she still makes it harder, doesn't she? Rick questioned, almost in pleading.

"It only seems that way because you find it easier to sin toward those who sin toward you. But it is your sin, not theirs, that is the source of your struggle. Carol cannot keep you from me. Only you can."

This voice came from within, but it was not his own, nor was it his grandfather's. It was a laser shot of light that came from somewhere else.

"Your love faileth. Mine never will. Come, cast off your sins and drink of my love."

Rick sat stunned on the kitchen floor. It had been years since he had been addressed so directly by the Spirit, and he had almost forgotten what it felt like.

So if I find it difficult to come to the Lord, it is because of my own sins. Rick pondered on that truth, and he realized that that was what his grandfather had taught him. His children loved fully, despite the problems he and Carol were creating, because of their own purity from sin. And Christ, who suffered at the hands of every soul, nevertheless loves us perfectly, and this because he was perfectly free from sin himself.

Rick looked down at the notes he had written:

4. I can recover mercy by remembering (a) Abigail's offering, (b) the Lord's question to Jonah, and (c) my own sins, the memory of which brings me to the Lord and invites me to rediscover his mercy and peace.

My own sins . . . he repeated to himself. *What sins are keeping me from Carol and therefore from the Lord? Well, they all are, I suppose.*

"Yes, they are, Ricky," came a voice, "but do you understand how they are doing that?"

Grandpa Carson was sitting at the head of the kitchen table.

18

CHAINS

"You weren't expecting me again?" Grandpa asked when he saw the look of astonishment in Rick's eyes.

"Well, not in my *kitchen*."

Grandpa smiled. He was holding a very old and very large book, which he extended to Rick, opened to a particular page.

"There is something I would like you to read," he said.

Rick stood up and joined him at the table. On closer inspection, "old" didn't adequately describe the book. It was in perfect condition, as if new, but at the same time it looked age- less, timeless.

"Go ahead, look," implored Grandpa Carson.

The large pages were made of a kind of paper Rick had never encountered, if they were made of paper at all. The pages were soft to the touch, and so light they seemed almost to float.

In this respect, they were almost feather-like. Yet they were at the same time so crisp, substantial, and weighty that Rick had the impression that no wind of this world, however strong, could rustle even a page.

As Rick looked down at the page, two things were very curious. First, although the page appeared to be thinner than any found in an average book, to the eye it looked to be of infinite depth, as the words seemed to float on the surface of an entire cosmos. Second, a line on the upper left illuminated itself and appeared to swim almost off the page. *Or were the words swimming away from him, down into the depths of the page?* Rick wasn't sure, but the sentence caught his eye and captured his attention, and as he started to read, he felt himself being pulled into it—either into the passage, or what was beneath it, or both.

Wo, wo be unto the inhabitants of the earth, it read.[50]

The words were physically tugging at him, as if he were tethered to them, like a car on a train that dutifully followed the line in front of it. He rushed to meet the page (or else the page rapidly engulfed the room; he wasn't sure which), and presently it felt as if he had joined the passage, and with it had plunged into the great beyond beneath the words. The words now presented themselves to him, and reading was no longer necessary, at least not reading as he had ever known it. He could feel, hear, and almost touch the words. They pulsed with life and were

CHAINS

everywhere around him, yet they directed his mind to something beyond—something that was slowly coming into focus.

The words continued—

And he beheld Satan; and he had a great chain in his hand, and it veiled the whole face of the earth with darkness.[51]

Rick now saw a great shadow below him, a darkness that chilled him to the bone, and a being whom Rick could only describe as anger personified, his hair and eyes jet black, his face pulled tight in an evil smile. In his hands he held a chain, each link larger, darker, and more foreboding than the one trailing it. But far in the distance, eons farther than Rick's eyes normally would have seen, Rick could see that the distant parts of the chain looked not to be a chain at all, but a silken cord—fine, soft, and inviting.

He leadeth them by the neck with a flaxen cord, spoke the words around him, *until he bindeth them with his strong cords forever.*[52]

This was a snare of the adversary, which he has laid to catch this people, that he might bring you into subjection unto him, that he might encircle you about with his chains, that he might chain you down to everlasting destruction, according to the power of his captivity. . . . And then they are taken captive by the devil, and led by his will down to destruction.[53]

141

Rick suddenly plunged into the darkness beneath him. He found himself on the earth among throngs of people in a great mist of darkness. Some were laughing, others crying, still others walked in grim silence. All, however, were moving, even those who thought they were not. The mist was moving, and all within it were moving as it moved. It was all very curious, as if the people were embedded within the mist—*part of it,* as it were—and so moved in unison with it.

Why don't they struggle against it! Rick wondered. *Why do they simply follow?*

> *If therefore the light that is in thee be darkness, how great is that darkness!*[54] came the words. *This is what is meant by the chains of hell.*[55]

> *For behold, at that day shall [the devil] rage in the hearts of the children of men, and stir them up to anger against that which is good. And others will he pacify, and lull them away into carnal security. . . . And thus the devil cheateth their souls, and leadeth them away carefully down to hell.*[56]

Rick looked intently at the throng. Here and there he noticed the soft fluttering of the flaxen cord he had seen a few moments earlier, lighting on the people before him like the line of a master fly fisherman. The people never flinched under the cord's touch. They appeared to be unaware of its presence.

Rick focused more intently and noticed, to his astonishment, that the mist of darkness was made up entirely of this cord as it swirled in and around the children of men. Above his head, the fluttering, gray mists darkened steadily until they gathered as one into a funnel of metallic darkness in the skies overhead, ending finally in the grip of the great hand he had seen earlier.

And [Satan] looked up and laughed, and his angels rejoiced.[57]

"No!" Rick yelled to the masses, as he began to run toward them. "Wake up!"

At the same moment, the words of the book cried to the throngs as well,

Awake! Awake from a deep sleep, yea, even from the sleep of hell, and shake off the awful chains by which ye are bound, which are the chains which bind the children of men, that they are carried away captive down to the eternal gulf of misery and woe.[58]

For the kingdom of the devil must shake, and they which belong to it must needs be stirred up unto repentance, or the devil will grasp them with his everlasting chains—from whence there is no deliverance—and they perish.[59]

"Do you know the meaning of what you are seeing?"

Rick started at the voice, which belonged to his grandfather, who was standing beside him.

"They're headed to their spiritual deaths, Grandpa," Rick exclaimed, gesturing to the masses, "and they don't even know it! They won't listen. They won't hear."

"You are quite right, Ricky."

"But why?"

"You tell *me*, Ricky. Why don't *you* listen? Why don't *you* hear?"

"What do you mean?"

His grandfather swept his arm as if to dismiss the throngs in front of him, and suddenly they were back in Rick's kitchen. He and Carol were in the middle of the argument they had had just that morning. Rick grimaced as he watched how he had acted and heard what he had said. It was all the worse having to witness it with his grandfather beside him. After Carol stomped her way up the stairs, his grandfather turned to him, his look solemn—not with disappointment but, it seemed to Rick, with love.

"You know better than that, Ricky, yet you still did it. In fact, at the time, you felt fairly compelled to say what you did, didn't you, despite what we have seen and heard together."

It was true. From the moment Rick ascended the stairs to see Carol, to the moment she stomped away in fury, Rick had felt out of control, almost as if he lacked the capacity to choose another way—to choose civility, calm, and compassion.

"There is a reason you felt that way, and a reason you find it near to impossible to follow the notes you wrote on that paper in your back pocket."

Rick was very interested in what his grandfather would say next, and he unconsciously leaned forward in anticipation.

"If you had looked more closely, Ricky, you would have seen yourself among the throngs you just witnessed, just as you saw yourself among David's men in the wilderness of Paran."

Rick's face showed surprise.

"You have just been shown your own predicament, Ricky. The flaxen cords have been caressing you for years. They have been wrapping themselves around your thoughts, your feelings, your memories, your desires. Having indulged them—having even been flattered by them—you have offered another the reins of your heart."

A cold chill ran down Rick's spine that reminded him of the shrill laughter he had heard when Satan and his hosts rejoiced at the plight of man.

"How can I escape them?" Rick asked earnestly, almost in a whisper.

"By following your own counsel—by waking up. By shaking off the awful chains with which you are bound."

"But how can I do that?"

Grandpa gave Rick a long look. "Perhaps we should work first on understanding what they are and how they are forged."

"Teach me, Grandpa. I want to know."

Rick's earlier resistance and defensiveness were gone.

Now, he just wanted to understand.

19

AGENCY IN THE BALANCE

You have been taught well by your parents about the pre-mortal life of man, and how there was a great battle in heaven between those who followed the Father's plan, led by Jehovah, and those who lined up with the dissenter, Lucifer."

Rick nodded.

"Do you remember what the battle was about?" his grandfather asked.

"Of course. Two things, really—Satan's pride and the agency of man."

Grandpa Carson waited for more.

"The plan for salvation was to provide mankind with bodies and afford us the opportunity to grow to become like our Heavenly Parents. We were to come to an earth, our minds veiled from the specific memories of our prior existence, to see if we would follow our spiritual intuitions and, through faith, learn to obey the commandments of God.

"Lucifer wanted to deny us our agency," Rick continued. "That is, he wanted the power to lead us at his will, to *make* us do what we needed to do to receive salvation. And then he wanted the glory for leading the effort. Many of the hosts of heaven joined him in this battle against Jehovah, Michael, and the other spirit children of God. Moses, Isaiah, and John the Revelator all speak of this."

"Good, Ricky. Let me ask you a question, then. You say that this premortal battle was over *agency,* and you are right about that. But what would you say agency is?"

"The ability to choose."

"The ability to choose *what?*" his grandfather responded.

"Isn't it just the ability to choose between options, and to be able to make those choices ourselves, without duress?"

His grandfather began fingering through the book Rick had just been reading. "Those who have been imprisoned," he said, "those who are handicapped, those who are poor—there are many things they cannot choose to do. Does that mean they then lack agency?"

"No, I don't think I would say that," Rick answered thoughtfully. "They all still have the ability to choose, even though their options may be limited."

Grandpa Carson put his thumb in the book, apparently to

save his place. "I want to push your thinking for a moment, Ricky," he said.

"Okay."

"Suppose a man is tied up so tightly he can't move a limb. Suppose as well that his eyes are propped open and his mouth is taped shut. All he can do is sit; he has no other options. Would he lack agency, the way that term is used in the scriptures?"

Rick considered this carefully. "I suppose so, yes."

"Really?"

"I suppose you'll say he wouldn't."

Grandpa Carson smiled at the friendly joust.

"That's correct, Ricky—that *is* what I would say. This man would have as much agency as the freest man on the street. The reason why is that agency does not refer broadly to the ability to choose—our choices are always bounded by certain limitations, after all. Rather, agency has to do with a particular kind of choice. Agency, as used in the scriptures, is the capacity to choose who we will follow—the Lord of Light or the Lord of Darkness. That is the choice that was at stake in the premortal realm. And it is a choice we retain here, even when bound and gagged."

"Okay," Rick offered pensively, unsure where his grandfather was going with his line of thinking.

"Actually," Grandpa Carson continued, "it is a choice we *may* retain, even when bound and gagged, for we can exercise our agency in such a way that we end up losing it as well. Part of having agency is having the agency to give it away."

"How can we give it away?"

"By giving Satan such iron hold upon our hearts that nothing but the merits of the Son of God can break us free," Grandpa answered.

Rick stood deep in thought, trying to process the implications, but his grandfather quickly continued.

"The war over agency did not end in the premortal world, Ricky. Satan took up the same war before a tree in Eden, a war that continues to this day, and a war most of mankind is losing.

"Here," he said, offering Rick the book again. "Read."

And there was war in heaven, the book began. *Michael and his angels fought against the dragon; and the dragon fought and his angels, and prevailed not.*[60]

This time, the words buried themselves deep within Rick and spoke directly to his soul.

Wherefore, because that Satan rebelled against me, and sought to destroy the agency of man, which I, the Lord God, had given him, and also, that I should give unto him mine own power; . . . I caused that he should be cast down. And he became Satan, yea, even the devil, the father of all lies, to deceive and to blind men, and—the words boomed within him—*to lead them captive at his will, even as many as would not hearken unto my voice.*[61]

Then Rick heard what he had heard earlier: *This is what is meant by the chains of hell,*[62] and he perceived once more the great chain that darkened the earth.

Rick looked up from the page. "So Satan still tries to control us, to lead us captive—that's what you mean, isn't it?" But Rick didn't wait for a response. "And that's what I saw earlier," he added, "the throngs of men being led captive at his will—bound by his cord and chain."

"Yes, Ricky. Satan's premortal plan for mankind was to lead us captive at his will in order to save us. After being cast down, his plan became to lead us captive at his will in order to destroy us. In its essence—the destruction of our agency through the capture of our wills—his plan hasn't changed from the beginning. The cord and chain you have seen—and your own life—are the proof of it."

Rick, who had been standing where he had observed his own argument with Carol, collapsed onto the chair beside him. "What do you mean, 'my own life is the proof of it'?"

"You and Carol are barreling toward an unthinkable end, each so committed to the justice of your own course that you are refusing to turn until too late—isn't that what you thought to yourself just last night?"

Rick remembered thinking that, although he couldn't quite place when.

"Your feelings toward her have turned cold, as have hers toward you. Yet each of you feels at a total loss to change those feelings. You are no longer sure if such a change is even possible, the indifference sweeps over you so quickly and so fully. When you heard her steps in the kitchen this morning, it was like the whole atmosphere of your morning changed. Just her presence darkened your mood. Am I right?"

Grandpa Carson looked seriously at Rick, who kept his eyes on the floor.

"If that isn't proof of the loss of agency and the chains of sin, what is? You're locked into a kind of insane death spiral— another of your own terms, I believe. Your every thought and feeling about Carol is taking you closer to the disaster you at once are denying and making inevitable. All the while, you feel that your feelings and thoughts are thrust upon you. What happened in this kitchen this morning was just the latest episode in that tragic story. Satan has hold of your heart, my boy, and he desires to destroy you."

Rick sat silently in the chair, covering his face with his hands. His grandfather was right, of course. He did feel out of control, as if his thoughts and feelings, however bitter and troubling, were thrust upon him. That had been a large part of his despair. "But how does he do it, Grandpa? How does Satan capture our wills and take our agency?"

"Read on," Grandpa Carson said, extending him the book once more.

Wherefore, it came to pass that the devil tempted
Adam, and he partook of the forbidden fruit and

transgressed the commandment, wherein he became subject to the will of the devil, because he yielded unto temptation.[63]

Because he yielded unto temptation—Rick repeated to himself, pondering the implications. "Adam became subject to Satan's will because he yielded to temptation?"

"Yes," his grandfather responded. "And remember the words you read just a minute ago as well: Satan leads captive at his will those who *'do not hearken unto the Lord's voice.'*[64] It is Satan's will that we not follow the Lord, and he attempts to capture us by enticing or tempting us to act contrary to the Lord's will, just as he did in the Garden with Adam and Eve. When we do that, he gains control over us and we effectively hand our agency over to him."

"But how does that happen? I don't understand how a single act of sin can capture us and subject us to Satan in the way you're describing. If that were the case, we'd *all* be subject to his will."

"And we are, Ricky. That's just the point. We *are* subject to his will. Think about it. Do we always do what we know we should? Do we love, or forgive, or pray like we know we should?"

Rick shook his head. "No," he said sullenly.

"So you see, Ricky, we *are* subject to his will. Even in the face of knowledge, we choose *away* from the Lord. We find ourselves falling away from the diligent living of his commandments, and from the *desire* to fully live them. 'Whosoever committeth sin,' the Savior declared—and that includes everyone—'is the servant of sin.'[65] And we 'receive our wages of whom we list to obey.'[66] Each sin makes us more susceptible to Satan's will because each sin is a capitulation to his will.

"Consider the terrible irony," he continued. "We fought a battle in the heavens in order to protect this precious commodity of agency—a commodity so important we were willing to cast out many of our spirit brothers and sisters to retain it—and then, as if we were central characters in a Greek tragedy, we come to this earth and exercise that agency in a way that effectively gives it away."

"But that's the part I don't understand. I don't understand how a single act of sin gives Satan control over us."

"That is because you misunderstand the nature of sin."

20

OF SIN

You've never been a smoker, Ricky, but knowing what you know about smoking, what do you suppose is one of the biggest problems with smoking a single cigarette?"

"The danger that it will hook you into more cigarettes."

"Exactly. How about with alcohol—what is one of the gravest dangers in a single drink?"

"The same. It would be the danger of getting hooked on additional drinks."

"Drugs, pornography? How about for them?"

"Same thing. One dose of anything like that makes further doses more likely."

"Why is that, do you suppose?" Grandpa asked.

"Well, they're addictive. I'm no expert on the body chemistry of addictions, but evidently each of those things changes the body somehow, or else somehow corrupts the spirit, so that you start to crave more of them."

"Yes. So with smoking or drinking or drugs or pornography, can you see how one act of sin can begin to give Satan power over you to lead you captive at his will?"

"Yes, with those kinds of acts, I can see that, yes."

"What if the same thing were true of any kind of sin?"

"Are you saying that it is?"

Grandpa Carson handed Rick the book. He took it in his hands and started reading, beginning where his grandfather was pointing.

And now, my sons, the passage began.

Once again Rick felt drawn in by the words. There was a rush of wind, and presently he found himself in a lush, forested land. The air was sultry, and perspiration beaded on his skin almost in an instant. He was on a hillside, with green rugged mountains rising directly behind him to the east. No more than a half mile to the west, the ocean shimmered under a setting sun, which painted the occasional clouds in pinks and purples. He was still holding the book, which felt heavy in his grasp.

Below him in a clearing sat ten or so men. A frail white-haired man, with a staff in his hand, sat at the front of the gathering, next to an altar of stones. It was he who was speaking.

Men are free according to the flesh, his words continued, *and all things are given them which are expedient unto man.*

And they are free to choose liberty and eternal life, through the great Mediator of all men, or to choose captivity and death, according to the captivity and power of the devil; for he seeketh that all men might be miserable like unto himself.[67]

"The great patriarch Lehi from the Book of Mormon," came his grandfather's voice, just behind him and to his left. "On the eve of his death, he is teaching his six sons, the two sons of Ishmael, and the former servant, Zoram, just what we have been talking about—that agency is the capacity we have to choose to follow either the Lord or the devil, *and* that if we choose against the Lord we lose our liberty and enter into the captivity of the devil."

And now, my sons, Lehi continued, *I would that ye should look to the great Mediator, and hearken unto his great commandments; and be faithful unto his words, and choose eternal life, according to the will of his Holy Spirit; And not choose eternal death, according to the will of the flesh and the evil which is therein, which giveth the spirit of the devil power to captivate, to bring you down to hell, that he may reign over you in his own kingdom.*[68]

"Notice what Father Lehi says, Ricky," his grandfather called to him, pulling his mind from the scene. "When we fail to follow the will of the Holy Spirit, we grant Satan power to captivate us through corruptible elements within our bodies— just as the addict loses control to his physical addictions. Sin is an addictive substance, Ricky. Our bodies can become wired for it. That is what Father Lehi is teaching his sons."

"But how?" Rick was still struggling to understand.

"Let's go back to the beginning."

The pages of the book in Rick's hand started to flip as if blown by a breeze, although Rick couldn't feel anything. Within seconds, the book fell open to a page near the beginning.

"Read," his grandfather commanded.

> *Wherefore, it came to pass,* Rick read, *that the devil tempted Adam, and he partook of the forbidden fruit and transgressed the commandment—*

He looked up at his grandfather. "I've already read this."

Grandpa Carson looked slightly cross. "Read, Ricky."

> . . . *wherein he became subject to the will of the devil,* Rick continued, *because he yielded unto temptation.*[69]

At this point the lush, tropical scene vanished and Rick found himself bathed in light. He read on, and a soothing voice descended from the heavens:

> *And I, the Lord God, called unto Adam, and said unto him: Where goest thou?*
>
> *And he said: I heard thy voice in the garden, and I was afraid, because I beheld that I was naked, and I hid myself.*
>
> *And I, the Lord God, said unto Adam: Who told thee thou wast naked? Hast thou eaten of the tree whereof I*

commanded thee that thou shouldst not eat, if so thou shouldst surely die?

And the man said: The woman thou gavest me, and commandest that she should remain with me, she gave me of the fruit of the tree and I did eat.[70]

"Ricky," came his grandfather's voice, pulling his mind from wherever it had been taken. "Who transgressed the commandment?"

His grandfather was standing next to him in the light.

"Adam did."

"Having transgressed the commandment, there is only one way back to God for Adam. What is that way?"

"Through Jesus Christ."

"Yes. But what must Adam realize after his transgression in order to come to Christ?"

"He had to know or be taught about Christ, to begin with."

"Yes. And then what?"

Rick thought for a moment. "I'm not sure."

"He needed to realize he had committed a transgression, Ricky, so that he would feel the need to come to Christ to be forgiven for it."

"Okay, I understand that."

"Do you?"

"I think so."

"Then read once more Adam's response to the Lord's query."

Rick read from where his grandfather was pointing.

And I, the Lord God, said unto Adam: Who told thee thou wast naked? Hast thou eaten of the tree whereof I commanded thee that thou shouldst not eat, if so thou shouldst surely die?

And the man said: The woman thou gavest me, and commandest that she should remain with me, she gave me of the fruit of the tree and I did eat.[71]

"What do you notice about Adam's answer, Ricky?"

"It isn't really an answer to the question, is it?"

"Go on," his grandfather encouraged.

"Well, the Lord asked Adam a straightforward question: 'Did you eat the fruit that I forbade you to eat?' And rather than just saying 'Yes,' Adam felt the need to say: 'Well, you gave me Eve and told me to stay with her, and she gave the fruit to me.'"

"Yes, Ricky. And notice how Eve did a similar thing. Read on."

And I, the Lord God, said unto the woman: What is this thing which thou hast done?

And the woman said: The serpent beguiled me, and I did eat.[72]

"What does it mean, Ricky?"

Rick pondered the question while his grandfather waited.

"In a way," Rick began, "Adam and Eve didn't think they had done wrong—or if they had, they felt like it was somehow okay or at least less bad because someone else caused or provoked them to do what they did."

"Sound familiar?"

"What do you mean?"

"Aren't you, in your relationship with Carol, exactly like Adam and Eve?"

Rick fell silent at the thought. He was beyond trying to defend himself.

"And if Adam is in any way unclear about the responsibility for his transgression, is he now going to be more or less likely to feel the need to come to the Savior?"

"Less," Rick answered.

"So notice, Ricky: One transgression, one choice away from the Lord, and what happens? The transgressor becomes blinded to his responsibility for sin, and he begins to fall into the captivity of the devil, which are the chains—the chains of sin—that keep him from feeling the need or desire to return to the Savior. This is how we become subject to the will of the devil when we yield to temptation."

Grandpa Carson took the book back from Rick.

"Now, Ricky, a few minutes ago I suggested that you misunderstood the nature of sin. Let me tell you what I meant by that."

"I think I already know," Rick interrupted.

"Go ahead, then. What are you thinking?"

"Something about sin changes us, kind of like bodily addictions do. We view the world differently after we sin than before. Like Adam, we become more concerned with ourselves and with how we look, and we somehow lose sight of the Lord and our need for him. We begin to see the world in ways that excuse our indiscretions. And then, like a kind of addiction, I suppose, we find it easier to continue in sinful paths. In fact, after Adam and Eve's transgression, Satan was able to get them to do something that never would have entered their minds before—to hide from the Lord."[73]

Rick was surprised by the words he heard himself saying—surprised in the sense that he found himself learning as he heard his words, if they were *his* words at all. These were new thoughts to him, yet they were coming from his mouth, and he felt a calm conviction within his breast as he spoke.

"It's interesting that Adam remained clear on *Eve's* need for the Savior," Rick mused. "He retained the ability to recognize *others'* sins. And yet even this ability became perverted, for he began to see others' sins as somehow an exoneration of his own. This kept him from fully contemplating his own sins and therefore kept him from turning fully to the Savior—or at least, it would have. I can't remember the particulars of the story well enough, but Adam and Eve were rescued from this blindness fairly quickly, I think. For they came to the Lord."

"Yes, Ricky, they did. But only after the Lord came looking for them.[74] They had turned their path from him and were hiding from his presence before he came and called out to them.

"And then," his grandfather continued, "remember what the Lord did next: He cursed the ground 'for their sake' and 'greatly multiplied' their sorrow in bringing forth children.[75] That is, he banished them to an earth where everything would be difficult—a curse that was 'for their own good' since the sheer difficulty of life would push them to look heavenward for help even in the midst of their sins, every such approach to the Lord providing them an opportunity to be saved from their captivity in sin."

Rick had never heard that idea before, and it fascinated him. *The difficulty of life itself is a blessing!* he realized. *For it initiates a desire within us to come to the Lord—a yearning we can feel even when we are blinded by sin!*

"The predicament of sin, then, Ricky, is much bigger than the fact that we commit individual sinful acts. It is that by so doing, we corrupt our hearts and become sinful ourselves—hard-hearted, stiff-necked, dark. We no longer see clearly but, as Paul warned, 'through a glass, darkly,'[76] which is according to Satan's plan to 'blind the eyes and harden the hearts of the children of men.'[77] The scriptures declare that this is 'a snare of the adversary, which he has laid to catch this people, that he might bring you into subjection unto him, that he might encircle you about with his chains, that he might chain you down to everlasting destruction, according to the power of his captivity.'[78]

"Once sinful in our hearts, acts and thoughts that were formerly reprehensible to us become desirable. We come to desire to do what we shouldn't and lose our desire to do what we should. Struggling with our own 'beams,' as we discussed before, we begin to become obsessed with others' 'motes.'[79] In the words of Paul, we 'think ourselves something'—better than, more deserving—when 'we are in fact nothing,' and are therefore 'deceived' about our sinfulness.[80] Paul called this 'the bondage of corruption.'[81] Losing sight of our sinfulness, we lose sight of our need for the One who has come to heal the sinner. Like Laman and Lemuel in the Book of Mormon, being hard in our hearts, we 'do not look unto the Lord as we ought.'[82]

"This, Ricky, again, is what is meant by 'the chains' or 'captivity' of sin: Precisely when we are most sinful and therefore most in need of repentance we least feel the desire or need to repent. This is the predicament of sin. And this is why the Lord himself declared, 'I require the hearts of the children of men,'[83] and why the prophets have uniformly declared that what is required is not just a cessation of sinful 'acts,' but a 'mighty change in our hearts.' It is as the prophet Alma taught: Only this mighty change of heart can loose us from the chains of hell."[84]

Grandpa Carson stopped for a moment and looked kindly at Rick. "You have a wonderful summary of some learning in your back pocket there, Son," he said, nodding toward Rick's hip. "Unfortunately, knowledge for the mind is never by itself enough to break from the chains of sin. Such knowledge can be helpful, to be sure, but only if it leads you to him who is powerful to save. Salvation is not in a sentence, or in a string of sentences, however profound. It is rather in a person—in the Messiah, come to earth, to deliver man from his sins."

21
—

OF REPENTANCE

The light slowly faded from around them, and Rick found himself, as he was before, sitting at his kitchen table.

He began to weep.

These tears were different, both in volume and feeling, from the torrential tears of self-pity and anger on the night Carol asked him to leave. They were rather the tears of awakening—cleansing, purifying tears. He was neither angry with Carol nor sorry for himself. On the contrary, he was beginning to feel sorry for Carol because of his own hard-heartedness. The pain he was feeling was bitter, to be sure, but he could taste a tinge of sweetness in it as well, for the tears were expelling his bitterness and giving room for the sweet feelings he had once known.

"So how can I get out of the mess I'm in, Grandpa? How

can I feel about Carol as I used to feel about her? How can I throw off these chains that hold me?"

"You are beginning to already."

"Really?"

"Yes. Can't you feel it?"

"Feel what?"

"Sorrow for how you have been toward Carol. Humility as you are beginning to realize that you lack the ability, yourself, to crawl out of the hole you find yourself in. A desire to repent, not just of unrighteous acts, but of an unrighteous heart. Openness to whatever may be required of you. Do you feel these things, Ricky?"

As Rick contemplated his grandfather's comments, he felt a soothing warmth inside him, like the outer rings of warmth one feels when approaching a campfire on a very cold night. As on such nights, Rick longed to move closer to the fire. "Yes, Grandpa, I do feel those things." And he sobbed all the harder at the realization.

"Oh, the wonder of God!" Grandpa Carson exclaimed, "and his goodness and mercy!"

"Gracious Father in Heaven," he continued, lifting his voice heavenward, "we thank thee for thy loving-kindness and tender mercies. We don't merit it, and never have, and yet still thou dost bless us with thy Spirit. We thank thee for this cleansing blessing, and approach thee in meekness and humility, and with deep gratitude.

"I love Ricky, dear Father. He is precious to me. Please sustain him in his pain that it may work to his salvation. May his heart break unto thee. May his contrition be true, and deep, and full. May he descend to the depths of humility. May thou show him the extent of his sins.

"Father, mayest thou put into him a new heart, according to thy promise to the meek and the lowly. Mayest thou take away the stony heart out of his flesh and grant unto him the pure heart and the peace that are promised to those who come unto thee. May he remember Abigail, and be able to extend mercy to Nineveh. May thy Spirit enter his and lead him in thy paths.

"Please be as well with Carol and the children. They are hurting and need thy sustaining hand. Bind up their wounds. Succor them in their sorrows. Hear the cries of the multitudes who hope for them and pray to thee on their behalf. Please, Father, I pray to thee with all the energy of my soul that thou wilt join this family together. Awaken within them the love they have known. Bring them back into each other's arms, and make their thoughts and feelings for one another sweet and holy.

"Dearest Father, we offer these yearnings in the name of thy Son. Through his mercies and merits we approach thee. And for his infinite atonement we praise thy holy name forever."

PART IV

THE MIRACLE OF GETHSEMANE

22
___

LIGHT IN THE DARKNESS

Grandpa Carson, his countenance shining with compassion, looked at Rick with understanding.

"You suffer, Ricky. Until now your suffering was in vain, for it was only for yourself. Now you suffer for others—for Carol, for your children, for all who are around you. You are pained by the pains they feel—the pains you have helped them to feel. Your heart is near to breaking.

"Blessed are you in this new suffering, for we truly are responsible one to another, just as you are now feeling. And our hearts must be broken in just this way, for we must be cured of the vanity of the sufficiency of our own hearts.

"As you come to feel fully responsible for the sufferings of those you love," he continued, "the Lord will take the pain of it from you. He has suffered everything, that we might be spared that fate.[85] Where the pain deserves to be, you will find his love in its place.

"Do you know the extent of his love, my son?"

"I don't believe I am worthy to."

Grandpa smiled. "For just that reason, you will know."

Rick suddenly found himself on a rocky hillside. Some fifty yards below he could make out the shapes of dozens of squat, ancient trees, their age evident in the gnarled shape of the branches that probed at the night air.

"The Garden of Gethsemane," spoke his grandfather beside him.

He continued: "After the Fall, the Lord said to Adam, 'As thou hast fallen thou mayest be redeemed,'[86] signifying the parallel relationship of the Fall and the Atonement. And so it is no accident that the Atonement will begin, as did the Fall, in a Garden. And it is no accident as well that the individuals in those gardens were each sinless, or that the events in those gardens centered on their exercise of agency—for Adam, whether he would partake of the bitter fruit, and for the Savior, whether he would partake of the bitter cup. The Savior and Adam faced a similar choice: If they did not partake, they would become lone men in paradise. Both partook that man might be. And by partaking of that bitterness, Adam came to know good and evil, and the Savior came to know all of the good and evil that had and would transpire in the hearts of men through all generations of time.

"And so, Ricky, you are about to witness an undoing of what had been done—a new exercise of agency, set in a garden, that rescues us from the captivity of sin, a captivity that entered the world through a prior exercise of agency in a garden of old. Agency will be redeemed tonight, and with it, 'all mankind, even as many as will.'[87] Because of the Lord's redemption, the children of men will be freed from the clutches of sin—'to act for themselves and not to be acted upon.'[88]

"Look."

Beyond the trees, and walking toward them, was a party of twelve. Only their cloak-draped outlines were visible under the blackened night sky. They carried no torches but seemed to know the path well, as none stumbled in the darkness. They walked in silence as they ascended stone steps that rose from the bottom of the valley below—the Kidron Valley, as Rick remembered. Across that valley, and set on the hill on the other side, stood the great walls of the temple and the holy city, Jerusalem.

Near the beginning of the ancient olive trees, One at the front of the procession gestured for the others to sit. Eight of them did so, while the first, and three others—Peter, James, and John, Rick knew from his study of these events—continued into the garden and among the trees. Rick strained for a look at them as their forms passed behind the branches and immense trunks for a good two hundred yards. Here, the Lord paused and turned to his companions.

What is it he said to them at this point? Rick strained to remember.

"'My soul is exceeding sorrowful, even unto death,'" his grandfather whispered. "'Tarry ye here, and watch with me.'"[89]

The figure who was Christ passed beyond his three disciples and from Rick's sight.

"'And he went a little further,'" came this voice from Rick's youth, now so soft it was almost inaudible, "'and fell on his face, and prayed, saying, O my Father, if it be possible, let this cup pass from me.'"[90]

And then his grandfather fell silent, and the night air stood still.

"What happens now is not for mortal eyes to witness," his grandfather said, in his more normal voice. "But it is most surely for human minds and hearts to understand."

"What do you mean, Grandpa?"

"Ricky, you need to understand what happens here tonight. Everything in your home, your heart, and your life depends on it."

"I think I understand, Grandpa. Here in Gethsemane, Christ pays for the sins of mankind. He suffers so terribly that blood runs from every pore."[91]

"Yes, Ricky, true enough. But how short that understanding still falls."

"Then tell me more," Rick pleaded. "What happens here tonight?"

"That is the beginning of it. It only happens here 'tonight' from the limited view of man."

"What do you mean?"

"I mean that our appreciation for what Christ did for us will fall abysmally short if we think that he fell on his face merely at the prospect of suffering for a few mortal hours, however excruciating that suffering might be. Both in impact, kind, and degree, what happens in Gethsemane cannot be marked merely by the clock of this fallen realm. Indeed, its impact could be felt from the days of Adam and Eve, even though by the reckoning of this earth it hadn't yet happened. The atonement happened as much outside this time as within it, though what was outside we cannot hope to grasp. It was and is an infinite and eternal act, unbounded by the limitations of mortality. No wonder the Savior trembled at the thought of it, and 'would that he might not drink the bitter cup.'[92] Mortal minds, with their earth-bound limitations, cannot comprehend the immensity of it."

Grandpa Carson paused for a moment to collect his thoughts.

"And what was the nature of that suffering?" he mused. "You say, 'He suffered for our sins,' but how glibly we can say it. Just what does it mean?

"Remember, the problem of sin is only partially that we engage in sinful acts. The far deeper problem is that by choosing to engage in sinful acts, our *hearts* become sinful. And when they do, Satan gains power over us to lead us captive at his will, to lead us into deeper and darker resentment, bitterness, anger, and sin. We become unclean, impure, corrupted—unable to abide the presence of God, in whose presence only the clean and pure can dwell. And we end up losing the very thing that is essential if ever we are to be able to be cleansed and find our way back to him: the desire and ability to choose to follow the Lord.

"Our hands are filthy from sinful acts, to be sure, Ricky, but our greater problem is that our hearts have become unclean as well. As Paul exclaimed, 'I delight in the law of God after the inward man: but I see another law in my members, warring against the law of my mind, and bringing me into captivity to the law of sin which is in my members. O wretched man that I am! who shall deliver me from the body of this death?'[93] If ever we are to stand in glory before the Father and the Son, the 'wicked spirit' that inhabits our hearts must, as the father of King Lamoni pleaded, be 'rooted out' of our breasts.[94] Unless someone can overcome for us the captivity of our hearts and make us free from our bondage to sin,[95] we will be damned forever."

"You're saying that's what the Savior did? What happened in the Garden of Gethsemane was that the Lord overcame the captivity of our hearts? That is what is meant by his 'paying for sin'?"

"Yes."

"But how?"

"How, indeed."

23

AN AGONY

R emember the Lord's teaching to Adam: 'As thou hast fallen thou mayest be redeemed.'[96] And remember how I mentioned earlier that, as this teaching implies, the atoning act that restores man's agency parallels the act that precipitated its loss. If that is true, and it is, then the Savior had to endure what Adam did after his Fall, and then redeem man from the effects of it."

"What does that mean, Grandpa?"

His grandfather looked solemnly at Rick. "In order to redeem mankind from the predicament of our captivity to sin," he began, "the Savior had to take upon *himself* that captivity—in its fullness—and then find a way to break free from it. Because of the power that Satan obtained through the Fall over the will of the flesh, man's agency could be redeemed only if all the powers of captivity that had been hardwired into the flesh by every sin of mankind could be overcome by an opposing power—by someone who could take our captivity upon him and yet escape from it, thereby providing a way of escape for *us*. This is what the Savior did, Ricky. In order to free us from the captivity of sinfulness, he took upon himself all the sins of mankind, the 'iniquities of us all.'[97]

"Do you understand what this implies?" his grandfather asked, an air of urgency in his voice.

At this point, Rick knew he had no idea.

"It implies that in order to redeem us from the chains of sin, the Savior had to take upon himself all of the chains that bind *us* to sin—in the words of Paul, to be 'in all points tempted like as we are.'[98] He had to shoulder 'the burden of the combined weight of the sins of the world'[99]—our sinful desires, our predispositions and addictions toward sin, our darkened hearts. The scriptures declare that he suffered as well everything that might *lead* us to sin—our 'pains and afflictions and temptations of every kind'[100]—so that 'he might blot out [our] transgressions according to the power of his deliverance.'[101] It was as Paul said: He 'who knew no sin' was 'made to be sin for us.'[102]

"With all of this sinfulness heaped upon him, he then had to withstand the unimaginable onslaught of the entire power and fury of the forces of hell, and do so, as Paul described further, 'yet [remaining] without sin.'[103] For Satan knew that if he could wield the power of his captivity—the chains of our sinfulness that lay ready to bind the Savior—and entice the Savior to sin, he would bring the Savior into his captivity as well. Then the destruction of agency would be complete, and mankind would be left without a way for their hearts to be purified and cleansed. There would therefore be no way for any of us to return to the Father, where only the clean and pure can dwell.

"Is it any wonder, Ricky, that Satan looked up and laughed when he held the entire earth in his chains?[104] On this night in Gethsemane, Satan is only one sin away from holding all creation in his hand."

Grandpa Carson looked grimly toward the Garden but couldn't hold the gaze. He turned his face away in pain.

"Even now," he whispered, a tear trickling down his cheek, "the powers of darkness are upon him in full force and fury. The term Luke used to describe this assault—the Greek word *agon,* translated as 'an agony'[105]—means, literally, 'a contest, struggle, or fight, facing an opponent.'[106] And that, my son, is what Gethsemane was. Or, rather," he said, glancing painfully again toward the Garden, "is. It is what latter-day prophets have referred to as 'indescribable anguish' and 'overpowering torture,'[107] a 'supreme contest with the powers of evil,' an 'hour of anguish when Christ had to meet and overcome all the horrors that Satan could inflict.'[108] And he suffers all this, Ricky—and never forget this—for *us.*

"This means that he is taking upon himself all the sinfulness of *your* heart, Ricky. You feel fairly compelled to argue with

Carol, to rage in your heart against her, to be soured by disappointment and despair. This night in Gethsemane, the Lord is taking upon himself all of the specific chains that bind and lead *you* captive. As he takes upon himself the desire to argue with Carol, and then breaks free from it, he will provide the way for you to break free as well. Your rage, your disappointment, your despair—the Lord will overcome all tonight and forge for you a new heart—clean, pure, undefiled, free.

"And he does the same for all—the addict, the abuser, the chronic complainer, those whose spirits are depressed. His struggle tonight is for all of mankind, but only because it was for each of us, individually and specifically."

Grandpa Carson paused for a moment, and the pain fled from his face. "But praise be to God!" he exclaimed, triumphantly. "The Savior has withstood in the aggregate what no man has been able to withstand individually: He refused to submit to Satan's will even though he was fully subject to it. Even with all of the mortal effects of our sins heaped upon and pulling at him, and with Satan and his hosts attempting to drag him down by that power to sin, the Savior was able to withstand and resist.

"The captivity of sin has been broken! The Lord God Almighty has risen 'with healing in his wings.'[109] He stretches forth his arms to the world, feeling after them with his Holy Spirit. He comes to each of us, posing the question he posed to Jonah, pleading with us, as Abigail did, to forgive, and literally dying to give us his Spirit and the new heart he has forged that will free us from the chains of our sins. If we harden not our hearts and stiffen not our necks against him, he will facilitate the breaking of our sinful, stony hearts and will give us what Ezekiel called his new 'heart of flesh,'[110] saving us from all our 'uncleannesses.'[111] This is the miracle of Gethsemane."

His grandfather's words filled Rick with gratitude and wonder. In all of his years attending Church and reading the scriptures, he had never really considered what it meant for Christ to suffer for our sins. And now that he had been given a glimpse of its meaning—however small a glimpse it was—he was overcome.

He stood shoulder to shoulder with his grandfather, looking out over the valley Kidron, too grateful to desecrate Gethsemane with his gaze.

24

RECOVERY

For ten minutes, grandfather and grandson stood quietly upon Olivet. For Rick, it was a time for reflection and commitment.

He understood perfectly well that the heart that needed replacing was his own. The Savior atoned for all of us, to be sure, but his grandfather had brought *him* to this hillside tonight. He felt, as all who come to the Savior do, that it was for his *own* sinful heart, above all, that the Savior was suffering, and for the raising of his own corrupt flesh to incorruption that the Savior would die on Calvary.[112] It was for this reason that he was overcome not only with solemnity, the way one might be when attending the funeral of a distant acquaintance, but with overflowing gratitude as well, the way Rick was at the funeral of the man he now stood beside—a funeral where he couldn't stop crying long after it was done, because of the depth of love he felt for him.

Among the many wonders of it all was this one: The Savior suffered an eternity's worth on account of Rick's bitter heart, but he loved him an eternity's worth in return. *How is it possible?* Rick wondered. *How is it done?*

"He is one with you, Ricky, that is the answer you seek."

"How is that the answer?"

Grandpa Carson now turned to look at him once more.

"When you tore your rotator cuff in college, Ricky, did you afterwards abuse your shoulder? By that I mean, did you get angry at it and treat it roughly?"

"Of course not."

"Why not? It was causing you pain."

"Because it was my own shoulder. What good would it do to hurt it further? I'd only be hurting myself."

And then it dawned on him what his grandfather meant.

We are one with our bodies, and for that reason, we don't react to a pain in a member of the body by inflicting that member with more pain. On the contrary, we dress it, and succor it, and nurse it back to health. If anything, we love most those parts of us that bring us the most pain. For they need us the most, and we, them.

"It is as if we are parts—" Rick whispered.

"Of the body of Christ," his grandfather said, completing the thought.

"Yes, the 'body of Christ,'" Rick repeated, lost in this thought.

"Read, Ricky."

His grandfather extended to him the book that he had read from before. Rick had not noticed it in his hands.

> *Husbands, love your wives,* he read, *even as Christ also loved the church, and gave himself for it; that he might sanctify and cleanse it with the washing of water by the word, that he might present it to himself a glorious church, not having spot, or wrinkle, or any such thing; but that it should be holy and without blemish.*
>
> *So ought men to love their wives as their own bodies. He that loveth his wife loveth himself. For no man ever yet hated his own flesh; but nourisheth and cherisheth it, even as the Lord the church: For we are members of his body, of his flesh, and of his bones.*
>
> *For this cause shall a man leave his father and mother, and shall be joined unto his wife, and they two shall be one flesh.*[113]

"After tonight, Ricky, you will have a greater understanding of these words. For the Lord took our infirmities—the infirmities of body and spirit—into his own body and spirit. We are one with him, not just metaphorically, but in actual fact. The scars man has given him bind us to his flesh for the eternities.

"Having become one with us, he takes our pains as his

pains. He nourishes and cherishes us. And this he does to sanctify and cleanse us, that we should be made holy and without blemish, as we must be if we are to live with his Spirit in mortality and dwell with the Father in the eternities.

"With Paul, I declare: 'So ought men to love their wives as their own bodies.' All of us at times create difficulty for our spouses and others, Ricky, as we've talked about before. And all of our spouses at times create difficulty for us, just as our joints sometimes ache and our limbs sometimes break. Here is how you will know whether you are one with your Carol: when, as you would for a limb or a joint, you cherish and nourish her when she is hurting. Do so, and you will feel nourished and cherished yourself."

Grandpa paused.

"It is time for me to return to your grandmother. I have been away, and I miss her so. I spent too many of our years separated from her under the same roof—married, but not one, Church-going, but rarely Christian."

"So what brought you together, Grandpa?" Rick asked sincerely.

"*He* did," he said, nodding toward the Garden.

"There was a period of our marriage that was very dark. And when I say a 'period,' I mean a period of *years*—perhaps as many as fifteen to twenty years. I felt neglected, taken advantage of, abused. And as time went on, I began to flirt with the idea of a life without her. *What would it be like? Surely it would be better.* I didn't really take the thought seriously at first, but I gave place to it, and it grew within me. As year stacked upon year, the thought grew sharper, and as it did, our life together grew worse. I tried to keep all this from the grandchildren, knowing how it would hurt them, and for the most part I thought I had succeeded—although you have taught me differently," he added, with a weak smile.

"Your parents knew about our struggles, however. And it was a good thing they did. One day, your father came looking for me out in the lower pasture. He had just been up at the house. Grandma was out, and he had happened to go into her sewing room to grab a pair of scissors. There in the drawer was a rather formal looking legal document. When he looked at it, he was shocked to discover a draft of divorce papers. Your grandmother was going to divorce me."

Rick felt like he had been knocked in the chest, the revelation stunned him so.

"This was news to me," his grandfather continued, "although when I heard it I wasn't entirely surprised. And in a way I think I even felt a little relieved. I was less emotional about it than your father would have liked, and he left frustrated and worried. I went back to my chores with a little extra vigor, reciting in my mind all the terrible things your grandmother had done to me over the years. The more I remembered the madder I became, until I was fairly chucking hay about in a rage.

"In the midst of it, however, something spoke to me. It

wasn't yet a voice, but I knew there was something untruthful in my rage—something overdone, something too convincing. Finally, I went into the barn and knelt to the earth. 'Why me, Father?' I cried. 'Why have I had to spend my years in such pain?'

"'You didn't have to,' came a voice.

"'What do you mean I 'didn't have to'?'

"'If you had come unto me,' the voice said, 'it all would have been different.'

"The words struck me like a thunderbolt, and I began to pray for more understanding. 'What do you mean, Come unto you? *What* would have been different?'

"What happened next I can't fully describe. A vision of sorts opened to me. I saw my life with your grandmother. As our days and years together raced before my eyes, I was shown something astonishing. I noticed a light that shone from us. Or rather, I noticed a light that *sometimes* shone from us—and sometimes more brightly than others.

"It was given me to know that we all shine forth a portion of the Lord's glory, and that we shine more brightly when we are living closest to him. Usually we do not perceive this light with our eyes, but you have felt it at times when you have been in the presence of saintly men and women—those who so fully reflect the Savior's light that it is tangible, if not visible, to those around them. To be in their presence is like being in the presence of a perfectly sung note. Their lives *resonate*. They pierce,

THE MIRACLE OF GETHSEMANE

they move, they motivate, they sing. And this because they live in tune with the Master.

"I noticed as I observed our lives that my light was growing dimmer. Something else that astonished me was that your grandmother's light was nearly always brighter than mine. This was particularly true in the moments I was most convinced of her inadequacy. Her light, too, was growing dimmer, however, with each succeeding year of our marriage, and at that moment, for the first time, I started to feel sorry. I broke down and cried as I hadn't in years.

"I was almost surprised to find how much all of a sudden I wanted to avoid divorce. I lifted my voice again to the heavens, this time begging for the Lord to save my marriage.

"'It is not your marriage that needs saving, Dale,' came the voice. 'It is your love.'

"'Learn to love Elisabeth with my love, and then, whether your marriage continues or not, you will have gained a companion.'

"'What do you mean, Lord?' I cried. 'But my marriage—'"

"'Your concern for your marriage is still a concern for self. Love Elly even if she chooses to divorce you. Then you will be married indeed.'"

Grandpa Carson became emotional at the memory. "My life has not been the same since that moment, Ricky, and I'd venture to say that neither has your grandmother's.

"We didn't divorce, thank the Lord, although it was touch

and go for awhile. But I felt the Lord's Spirit and sustaining strength through that time. And for a period of a week, I was still allowed to witness the light that shines from men. I saw it shining from my precious Elisabeth, dimmed by our mutual distress, but shining still, even when I walked into the house that day. This light brightened and sustained me.

"Do you understand, now, Ricky, why *I* was selected to meet with you?"

Rick nodded, his heart overflowing with gratitude for his grandfather's love, and with a new appreciation for his grandmother.

"I know your pain, Son. And having come together with Elisabeth, I know Carol's as well.

"But more than that, I know the joy that was forged in Gethsemane. I know the Savior's mercy and love. I have felt it, I have bathed in it, I have been saved by it. And I continue to be saved by it every day."

Rick was mildly surprised by this comment.

"You think because I have already died that I have no need for the Lord? The need for the atonement reaches far past the grave, Ricky. If I stand before you worthy, it is only because of the merits of the Son of God. I shudder in this place as well, for I know that it is for my sinfulness that the Lord is suffering."

Rick stood in silence.

"My prayer now is for you, my boy."

"Thank you, Grandpa," Rick said, choking out the words.

"Is there something that still troubles you?"
"Yes, one thing."
"What is it?"
"I'm afraid."

25

COVENANTS

O f what are you afraid?"

Rick thought of that morning with Carol. "Of my own sinfulness," he said. "Of the pull of the darkness within me. I'm afraid I won't be able to sustain the change you are talking about."

"You *won't* be able to, Ricky. Only One can sustain that change. If you remember that, your continued failures will lead to your salvation, and to the salvation of your marriage. In humility, you will ever return to the Lord. And being keenly aware of your own sins and shortcomings, you won't demand perfection of Carol either."

Grandpa Carson looked tenderly at Rick.

"Don't misunderstand, Son. The Lord does not give you a new heart only once. He gives you a new heart every time you come to him repentantly, in faith, believing that you will receive. We need the gift of a new heart every day."

"But will I be able to do that, Grandpa?" Rick whispered. "That's what has me worried."

"Do you recall in the Book of Mormon the people who were known as 'the people of Anti-Nephi-Lehi' or 'the people of Ammon'?"

"Yes. They were the Lamanites who accepted the gospel during the years the sons of Mosiah spent among them, preaching."

"That is correct. And after their conversion," Grandpa continued, "they each asked the same question you are now asking of me: 'How can I be sure that this mighty change within me will last?' They too were afraid. The reason they were afraid was that, like you, they knew their histories too well. They had been a war-mongering people that had delighted in shedding the blood of their enemies, the Nephites. For this they had sorely repented, and the Lord had cleansed and given them new hearts.[114] But they worried that they might stumble and darken their hearts with the sins that had darkened them before. 'Since it has been all that we could do,' their king declared to them, 'to repent of all our sins and the many murders which we have committed, and to get God to take them away from our hearts, . . . let us retain our swords that they be not stained with the blood of our brethren.'[115]

"And then do you remember what they did?"

Rick couldn't. "No," he finally said.

"The scriptures record that they gathered all their weapons of war and then, as a people, buried them deep in the earth and covenanted with God *and* with each other that they would never take them up again."[116]

Grandpa Carson looked at Rick. Why do you suppose they buried them 'deep' in the earth, Ricky? Why wasn't a shallow grave sufficient?"

"They probably were worried again by their history. If the grave was shallow, in a pinch they might have become tempted to take up their weapons in violation of the covenant they had made and risk a return to their old ways. They probably didn't want to take that chance."

"Exactly. And as things happened, they would have soon been so tempted. For their own people, the Lamanites, later came to war against them in order to destroy them, and the scriptures tell us that on one occasion 'they were about to take up their weapons of war' in response.[117] Good thing they were buried deep. Friends who knew of their history and of the covenant they had made to keep their hearts clean forbade them from doing it, and these friends, along with two thousand sons of the people of Ammon, took up arms to protect them.[118] These defenders had not in the past been corrupted with delight in the shedding of blood. They therefore were able to take up arms with the blessing of the Lord when war was thrust upon them, in order to protect their liberties, their families, and their faith—and to seek the same protections on behalf of the people of Ammon.[119]

"One of the most touching stories in all of scripture is the story of how many of their brethren, the Lamanites, were themselves converted to the Lord when the people of Ammon would not take up arms against them."[120]

Grandpa Carson paused to give Rick time to ponder the story.

"Hearkening back to the story of these people, at the end of the Book of Mormon the prophet Mormon declared: 'Know ye that ye must come unto repentance, or ye cannot be saved. Know ye that ye must lay down your weapons of war, and delight no more in the shedding of blood, and take them not again, save it be that God shall command you.'[121]

"Ricky, your problem has not been delight at the shedding of blood, but you have had other weapons in your marriage and have delighted in other sinful things. You wield cold silence. You complain. Your tongue has become sharp. You carry an air of superiority. No weapon is as devastating in a home as a heart that has stopped loving. There are other sins in your life too, not necessarily directed at Carol, that have held you captive."

Rick couldn't argue any of this and no longer had the desire to anyway.

"About these sins that have taken root in your soul, the Savior said, 'I give unto you a commandment, that ye suffer none of these things to enter into your heart; for it is better that ye should deny yourselves of these things, wherein ye will take up your cross, than that ye should be cast into hell.'[122] The Lord isn't saying that it will be easy, Ricky. In the beginning, he says, pulling free from the sinfulness that has kept us bound may well be like taking up a cross and carrying it on our backs. But by that image he reminds us that we are not in this alone and that we do not have to carry it forever, for One will take it from us and, with it, the burdens that weigh us down."

Grandpa Carson smiled kindly, yet gravely, at Rick.

"If you are worried about falling back into sin and the captivity that has held you fast," he continued, "and you do well to worry, then I would invite you to learn from the people of Ammon. Learn to bury your weapons of war—your sins—down deep, too deep to be retrieved when you might be tempted. And then covenant with God, Carol, and any others toward whom you have wielded those weapons, that you will never take them up again. And ask them to help you to keep this covenant."

His grandfather looked at him solemnly. "Will you agree with *me* that you will do this?"

"Yes, Grandpa, I will."

"Do this, Ricky, as the scriptures teach, with 'all the energy of your heart,' and you will be filled with the Lord's love—the love that never faileth."[123]

"Okay, Grandpa," Rick said earnestly, but still with trepidation. "I'll try."

"It's okay, even wise, to be afraid, Ricky. You should fear sin with all your soul, for it is the freedom of your soul that is at stake. To those who fear as they ought—like *you* do, like the people of Ammon did—the prophets declare: 'Be watchful unto prayer continually, that ye may not be led away by the temptations of the devil, that he may not overpower you, that ye may not become his subjects, and be led away captive by him.'[124] Arm yourself through prayer, Ricky. You are vulnerable. We all are. Let your desires for the Lord be your shield."

Rick took in a deep breath and looked up at his grandfather. For the first time during their meetings together, Rick felt real conviction—not the cocky confidence that covers and blinds one to sin, but rather the humbling recognition that sin is at the door, but that there is One more powerful than sin that guards the way if we will let him.

Grandpa gave Rick an encouraging smile. "I mentioned that the Lord granted me a gift during that critical week of my life. He allowed me to see the light that was shining from men."

Rick nodded.

"It is a gift I have received again since passing into this life, and I have come to know that light—or 'glory'—is the most distinguishing characteristic of man. I have seen Carol as she is, Ricky, in the fullness of her glory. You married a woman who is noble and great. You once knew this well, and still do, although you have too often forgotten it. But believe me when I tell you, you have hardly known a fraction of the truth concerning her. One day you will see her as she is, and on that day, you will be forever grateful that you heeded what you have written on that paper in your pocket."

Rick touched his hand to his hip pocket and felt the bulge of the paper within it.

"God bless you, my son. May you give away your sins to know him.[125] And to know Carol."

At that moment, the darkness of the night evaporated in a sea of light. Rick found himself sitting on the kitchen floor, his back to the cabinets, as he had been when his grandfather had first appeared at the kitchen table, this too having been a dream or vision. The paper of summary points was still in his hand.

He read what he had written once more. As he did so, he realized it was incomplete.

All of this is possible, he thought, *only because the Lord claimed our sinful hearts as his own, laid himself bare before the forces of evil, and through an eternity's worth of faithful suffering broke the chains of captivity for all who come to him with a broken heart.*

Rick looked heavenward, his soul overflowing with gratitude. As he did so, his thoughts turned (or *were* turned) to Carol. She was upstairs—in pain, likely crying. How sorry he was, now, for everything! And how petty his complaints now seemed.

He rose to his feet and quickly climbed the stairs. Unlike earlier that morning, his desire for her grew with each step. He had weapons to bury, covenants to make, and a bride to take into his arms.

He had never felt so unworthy of her love.

And for just that reason, he had never been so likely to receive it.

EPILOGUE

P erhaps you are wondering what happened.
      After Rick climbed the stairs, he apologized as he never
really had before, for he meant it in a deep way that he'd never
really felt before. No part of him apologized in order to extract
some confession or acknowledgement from Carol. Whether she
needed to apologize to him for anything was so far from his
mind and heart that the thought never occurred to him. All he
felt was sorrow and desire: sorrow for loving her less than she
deserved to be loved, for bringing her pain, for scarring her
soul; and desire to fill in whatever scars he had caused, no matter how long it took.

      Her response to his apology wasn't important. For once in
his life, he wasn't saying something to her in order to elicit a
particular response. He was simply loving her. He climbed the
stairs with no strings attached.

It wouldn't surprise you, would it, if Carol heard Rick's words skeptically? It wouldn't have surprised Rick either, given all the sour history they had shared. He fully expected Carol to reject whatever he said to her as just so many words. The prospect didn't bother him, for he knew that this time they weren't just words. How could he expect anything but skepticism after all the bitter words and looks he had hurled her direction?

How utterly surprised and humbled he was when she said, "You really mean it, don't you?"

"Yes, Carol, I do. I'm so sorry."

To which Carol then said, "Oh, Rick, I'm the one who needs to apologize."

It didn't have to be that way, of course. She could just as easily have said, bitterly, "Why should I believe you this time when you've never really meant it in the past?" Rick would have understood that, and in that moment, he wouldn't have loved her any less for it.

Of course, somehow, someway—for our own sakes—we, as Carol, need to accept the apologies of our Ricks. When we finally do, we will realize, as Carol did, that failure to receive an apology is something that needs repenting of as fully as failing to give one. It is the Savior, after all, who is apologizing. Rick was just giving voice to the feelings and words that the Lord formulated for him in Gethsemane.

How did Rick do after that initial apology? And how did

Carol do in response to him? It is tempting to think that these are the important questions, as if the rest of the story will tell us the remainder of what we need to know. But did we need to know Jonah's answer to the Lord's question?

What more do I need than knowledge of the atonement? What more do I need than to come to Him? What more do I need than a broken heart? What more do I need than his Spirit—the Comforter—which will teach me "all things what I should do"?[126]

The question for me is not what Rick said or did after he climbed the stairs and over the ensuing days and weeks. It is rather what I need to say or do after climbing the stairs in my own life. And then what I need to *keep* saying and *keep* doing.

"Should not I spare Rick?" "Should not I spare Carol?"[127]

This is what the Lord asks of us.

Since we *are* Rick and we *are* Carol, the Lord prays, for our sakes, that we will answer mercifully.

NOTES

1. John 14:6.
2. See D&C 112:13.
3. Luke 2:14.
4. Ephesians 2:14–15; emphasis added.
5. 1 Samuel 25:13.
6. See D&C 64:22.
7. See Matthew 23:25–28.
8. See 1 Samuel 25:14–19.
9. See 1 Samuel 25:20, 23.
10. 1 Samuel 25:24.
11. See 1 Samuel 25:25, 31.
12. See 1 Samuel 25:28, 31.
13. See 1 Samuel 25:32–34.
14. See 1 Samuel 25:35.
15. Luke 24:23.
16. See Luke 24:14–15.
17. Luke 24:17.
18. Luke 24:25–27.
19. Luke 24:36.
20. Luke 24:44.
21. See Luke 24:45.
22. See 2 Nephi 11:4.
23. See Genesis 45.
24. See Daniel 3.
25. See Mosiah 24:13–15.
26. See 1 Samuel 24, 26; 2 Samuel 1.
27. 1 Samuel 25:24.
28. See 1 Samuel 25:23–31.
29. 1 Samuel 25:28.
30. D&C 64:10.
31. 1 Samuel 25:31.
32. See 1 Samuel 25:28.
33. See Matthew 25:40, 45.
34. For events described in this chapter, see Jonah 1:1–15.
35. See Hosea 7:11; 8:9; 10:6; 11:11.
36. 2 Nephi 25:23.

37. See Matthew 20:1–16.
38. For events described in this chapter, see Jonah 3–4.
39. See Jonah 3:4–5.
40. Jonah 4:11.
41. Matthew 18:33–35.
42. Jonah 2:8.
43. Alma 41:10.
44. See Mosiah 4:1–3.
45. See Alma 36:16–21.
46. Alma 22:18.
47. Jonah 4:11.
48. See D&C 121:37.
49. See Matthew 7:3–5.
50. Moses 7:25.
51. Moses 7:26.
52. 2 Nephi 26:22.
53. Alma 12:6, 11.
54. Matthew 6:23; see also 3 Nephi 13:23.
55. Alma 12:11.
56. 2 Nephi 28:20–21.
57. Moses 7:26.
58. 2 Nephi 1:13.
59. Adapted from 2 Nephi 28:19, 22.
60. Revelation 12:7–8.
61. Moses 4:3–4.
62. Alma 12:11.
63. D&C 29:40.
64. See Moses 4:4.
65. John 8:34.
66. See D&C 29:45.
67. 2 Nephi 2:14, 27.
68. 2 Nephi 2:28–29.
69. D&C 29:40.
70. Moses 4:15–18; see also Genesis 3:9–12.
71. Moses 4:17–18; see also Genesis 3:11–12.
72. Moses 4:19; see also Genesis 3:13.
73. See Genesis 3:8; Moses 4:14.
74. See Genesis 3:9; Moses 4:15.
75. See Genesis 3:16–17; Moses 4:22–23.
76. 1 Corinthians 13:12.
77. 1 Nephi 13:27.
78. Alma 12:6.
79. See Matthew 7:3–5.
80. See Galatians 6:3.
81. Romans 8:21.
82. See 1 Nephi 15:3.
83. D&C 64:22.
84. See Alma 5:10–14.
85. See D&C 19:15–19.
86. Moses 5:9; emphasis added.
87. Ibid.
88. 2 Nephi 2:26.
89. Matthew 26:38.
90. Matthew 26:39.
91. See Luke 22:44; D&C 19:18.
92. See D&C 19:18.
93. Romans 7:22–24.
94. Alma 22:15.
95. See John 8:32–34.
96. Moses 5:9; emphasis added.

97. Mosiah 14:6; see also James E. Faust, "The Atonement: Our Greatest Hope," *Ensign,* November 2001, 18–20.
98. Hebrews 4:15.
99. Joseph Fielding Smith, *Doctrines of Salvation* (Salt Lake City: Bookcraft, 1954–56), 1:129; see also *Teachings of Ezra Taft Benson* (Salt Lake City: Bookcraft, 1988), 14–15.
100. Alma 7:11.
101. See Alma 7:13.
102. 2 Corinthians 5:21.
103. Hebrews 4:15.
104. See Moses 7:26.
105. Luke 22:44.
106. See Jack Welch, "Becoming a Gospel Scholar," *This People,* Summer 1998, 52.
107. James E. Faust, "The Atonement: Our Greatest Hope," *Ensign,* November 2001, 18; quoting John Taylor, *The Mediation and Atonement* (1882), 150.
108. See James E. Talmage, *Jesus the Christ* (Salt Lake City: Deseret Book, 1979), 613.
109. Malachi 4:2; see also 2 Nephi 25:13; 3 Nephi 25:2.
110. Ezekiel 36:26.
111. Ezekiel 36:29.
112. See 1 Corinthians 15:50–54.
113. Ephesians 5:25–31.
114. See Alma 24.
115. Alma 24:11, 13.
116. See Alma 24:17–18.
117. See Alma 56:7.
118. See Alma 56:8.
119. See Alma 43:45–47; 53:13–21.
120. See Alma 24:20–27.
121. Mormon 7:3–4.
122. 3 Nephi 12:29–30.
123. See Moroni 7:46–48.
124. Adapted from Alma 34:39; 3 Nephi 18:15.
125. See Alma 22:18.
126. See 2 Nephi 32:3.
127. See Jonah 4:11.